VALENTINE GEORGE

An ordinary man, who lived through extraordinary times.

PAT BACKLEY

VALENTINE GEORGE

Copyright ©2022 by Pat Backley

This book is a work of fiction. Any references to historical events, real people, or real places are used fictitiously. Other names, characters, places, and events are products of the author's imagination and any resemblances to actual events, places or persons, living or dead, is entirely coincidental.

All rights reserved. No part of this publication may be reproduced, distributed, or transmitted in any form or by any means, including photocopying, recording, or other electronic or mechanical methods, without the prior written permission of the publisher, except in the case of brief quotations embodied in critical reviews and certain other commercial uses permitted by copyright law.

Pat Backley
www.patbackley.com

Paperback ISBN: 978-0-4736180-5-6
EPub ISBN: 978-0-473-59902-7
Audiobook ISBN: 978-0-473-59904-1

Edited by Colleen Ward

Cover design and formatting by formattedbooks.com

CONTENTS

ACKNOWLEDGMENTS

This book is dedicated to my ancestors, most of whom I never had the chance to meet.

They were ordinary people living ordinary lives, and I am proud to weave some of their memories into my books and share them with the world.

They had no voice, so I will make sure their stories can be heard.

Of course, as always, I also dedicate this book to my beloved daughter, Lucy.

MORDEN, ENGLAND
FEBRUARY 1934

Valentine George slumped down into the old oak Windsor chair. It was the only stick of furniture remaining in the house.

He wept.

And wept.

And wept.

He stared at the battered old clock on the wall and watched the minutes as they ticked by.

And still, he wept.

Before he knew it, the light was going. It was a gloomy afternoon in mid-winter, so it got dark quite early.

Blinking through his tears, he noticed it was almost 2:30 p.m. He slowly and very reluctantly got out of the chair, walked into the shabby little kitchen, and put the kettle on to boil.

A few minutes later, the shrill whistling stirred him from his dark thoughts. The kettle had boiled and was telling him to get a move on.

If only he was all alone, he could end it all. There was plenty of rope in the cellar.

But he knew that wasn't an option.

They would be home from school soon–his two beloved children. Motherless yet again.

While he drank the strong sweet tea, he thought about the last few years.

He had been so happy; he thought she had been, too. Obviously, he had been wrong.

In an effort to cheer himself up, he thought about his childhood and the first time he ever drunk a cup of tea. He had been just five years old then; life had seemed so simple.

ONE ACRE COTTAGE,
ALTON, HAMPSHIRE,
ENGLAND
1899

"Now, now, Valentine, don't gulp it down like that! You'll burn your throat."

His mum, Martha, was always such a worrier.

Although he had been christened George Valentine, his mum always called him Valentine. She had argued for months with her husband over the name–he thought it was far too namby-pamby for a boy–but she loved it. She found it rather romantic and much more appealing than the sensible, but rather stuffy names her other boys had been given: Robert, Albert, John, Jack, and Edward, all named after their ancestors. She knew it was traditional to give children the names of other family members, but after bearing seven children, she felt justified in arguing to choose at least one of their names. George Valentine had been christened in the same little church as his siblings, the old stone church in the East

End of London, where generations of his mother's ancestors had been christened, married, and then buried in the little graveyard.

Prompted by his mother, he became known as Valentine George. Most people soon forgot that it had ever been the other way round; even Dad called him Valentine, eventually.

He was five years old and the youngest of Martha's seven children. She loved them all dearly and still tried to wrap them in cotton wool. It made his dad mad, especially when she fussed over his big brothers.

"For God's sake woman! You'll turn them into sissys, treating them so soft. The lad knows how to drink a cup of tea without burning himself."

His dad, Robert, spoke harshly, but really he was a gentle man, just a bit worn out from trying to keep his big family fed and clothed on a labourer's wage. He also understood why Martha was so protective of her children; two of their sons, Jack and Edward, had both died in infancy, both snatched away by tuberculosis. He remembered their last awful days–the night sweats, the blood-tinged coughing.

Robert hadn't always been a labourer.

He had been a bright boy, apprenticed at the age of 14 to the town clerk in the little market town in Hampshire, where he had grown up. He lived on the farm that had been worked by his family for generations. They were tenant farmers, each generation passing the space down to the next, and hundreds of his ancestors were buried in the churchyard nearby. He didn't want to work on the farm like his brothers and had been so happy to get the office job, but after a few years being stuck behind a desk doing menial paperwork, he became bored.

He wanted more from his life.

Thus, at the tender age of seventeen, Robert left his hometown, bound for the bright lights of London.

The first few years had been good.

He had found lodgings in an old tenement block in the East End, sharing with another couple of lads he knew from home. He landed a good job in the city working in the offices of a big printing company in Shoe Lane, off Fleet Street. He often walked to work, enjoying the stroll along the river, past the Tower of London and St. Botolph's Church. Many times he stopped to peer into the old graveyard, which was rumoured to be the burial place of Tudor rebels. He discovered a real love of history and enjoyed learning about the ancient buildings and alleys surrounding his new home. It was so very different to the life he had known growing up. In the country there had been no big buildings, no dark alleyways lit by gas lamps, no constant noise and crowds, no overpowering human smells. He often took a detour off Cable Street and down Graces Alley so that he could pass Wilton's Music Hall. Robert would peer into the dark, cavernous space, imagining how different and exciting it would have looked in its heyday. It had closed down in 1881 and was apparently going to re-open soon as the East London Methodist Mission.

Robert worked long hours and his boss was pretty unpleasant, but the job paid quite well—well enough for him to go out with his mates every weekend to the music hall, the pub, or dancing.

He was a good dancer; his mum had taught him how to waltz when he was just a young lad, whirling him round their big farmhouse kitchen.

"One, two, three, one, two, three."

"Just keep saying that in your head, lad, then you won't forget the steps. One, two, three, one, two, three."

He thought of her every time he danced with a young lady. They may be younger and prettier, but he had yet to find one who could dance as well as his old mum.

By the time Robert was twenty, he was well-established in his London life.

He had a good job, good mates, and plenty of pretty young girls who adored him. But even with all this, he wanted more.

Then one day, quite unexpectedly, he found her. His more.

He had gone to the music hall like he did most Saturday nights. He and his mates always sat in the gods–those were the cheapest seats. They were so high up that sometimes, you had to strain to hear what was being said on stage. But there were always plenty of pretty girls to look at up there. They all got all dressed up in their best, especially for a night out. He glanced around, taking in all their finery–the pretty lace collars brightening up their drab gowns, the multitude of fancy hats, some adorned with feathers, flowers, or even bunches of artificial fruit. He admired their beauty below the bonnets. And then, he caught one of them staring at him. She looked away quickly, embarrassed to be caught, but not before he had time to register that she was exceptionally attractive.

When the show was over he dawdled behind his mates, desperate to catch another glimpse of her. He hung around the foyer of the hall, staring at every girl who walked past.

"C'mon Rob, we want to try and get a pint in at the Rose and Crown before it shuts. Hurry up, man."

He had to admit defeat. It was too late, he had missed her.

For the next month he went to different music halls every single Friday and Saturday night hoping to see her, but she never appeared. He had all but lost hope. Then, coming out of the printers where he worked one wet and windy afternoon,, he saw her, crossing the road to catch the omnibus. He ran across the road too, intending to leap on board and surprise her, but he didn't make it on time; the bus pulled away. The next night he stood by the bus stop for two hours willing her to show up, but of course, she didn't.

The next weekend he went alone to the music hall, promising to meet his mates at the pub afterwards. That night, his waiting ended. She was there and she smiled at him!

He courted her for seven months.

Her name was Martha Patmore and she lived with her large family in Commercial Buildings, a rundown tenement just off Commercial Road in the East End. Her family was poor but very loving, and they soon accepted him. She had three elder sisters who worked at the Bryant and May Match Factory, and her four brothers all worked on the docks.

Martha had always known that she would rather die than join her sisters at the factory. It was such hard, dismal work. The girls who worked there all ended up looking grey and ill and often died way before their time, thanks to the constant inhalation of noxious fumes.

She decided when she was just seven years old that she wanted to be a dressmaker instead. She had spent hours with their neighbour, a Russian lady called Olga, watching her sew and learning how to make beautiful garments. Olga worked in her shabby little room by candlelight mostly, as the tenement had such tiny glass panes that barely any natural light could slip through the grimy windows. She made garments for the smart establishments of Bond Street–fancy showrooms where ladies would go to dress in the latest fashions and be fawned over. These ladies assumed that their new clothes would be made in smart workshops, hidden behind the glossy façade of the showroom, but they were wrong. Most of their fine dresses were sewn by hand by women like Olga, women living impoverished lives, wearing their fingers to the bone for a very small return while the owners of the dress shops made a very good profit off their labour.

Over the years, Olga had told little Martha her story. She and her parents and siblings had escaped from the pogroms in Russia, only to find themselves in the East End of London facing starvation. By the time Martha met her, Olga's parents were long dead, as were three of her sisters and one brother. They had all died of disease and despair, leaving only Olga and her youngest sister, Svetlana, to cope with life in this strange new land.

Svetlana grew to be very beautiful, but sadly, she had severe epilepsy. This meant Olga had never gone out to work; she never wanted to leave her sister alone in case she had a bad seizure. Instead, she took in piece work, sewing beautiful gowns for strangers–rich ladies she would never meet.

Martha loved Olga and Svetlana. To her, their lives seemed so different and colourful than hers. In their company, she saw beyond the dinge and grime of the little room. She saw instead, the steppes of Russia; she saw St. Petersburg, Kiev, and Odessa.

She learnt to sew. Olga taught her so well that when she was just thirteen years old, she was accepted by the big new department store, Selfridges in Oxford Street, as a junior apprentice in their workshop. For them she did alterations, took up hems, and added a dart or two here and there. It was simple, repetitive, and rather boring work, but Martha loved it. She was thrilled to have the job. The store was such an exciting place to work. Of course, as a mere apprentice, she was never allowed into the store itself–the closest she ever got was peering through the shop windows on her way home at night–but she knew how lucky she was. How lucky to have got a job "up West." A job that all her friends and her sisters envied. She was poorly paid, but the job gave her some sort of social standing; everyone thought she was very posh because she worked at Selfridges.

She was just seventeen years old when she met Robert. Robert, whom she realized very quickly was the love of her life. He treated her like a lady, not just a poor young girl from the slums. He courted her properly. For months, he would walk from Fleet Street to Oxford Street to meet her after she finished work. They would catch the omnibus home together and he would walk her right to her front door. He never tried to kiss her. He was always respectful, behaving like the perfect gentleman, and as he walked away, he always turned back and tipped his hat at her, a big smile on his handsome face.

It took him seven months to pluck up the courage to propose. Seven of the longest months when he longed to kiss her, but didn't, because he wanted it to be special. He didn't want to be just another suitor, another man who took what he wanted from a girl and then walked away. Even though it was 1887 at the time, he still had old-fashioned ideas–ideas that his mum had taught him about always behaving like a gentleman and treating every girl as if they were your own sister.

By the time he eventually plucked up the courage to ask Martha's dad for her hand in marriage, no-one was surprised. It had been obvious to everyone that he adored her, that he worshipped the very ground she walked on.

They decided not to wait. They were both desperate to be together, to start sharing their lives, so the church was booked and the banns were read. Martha planned to wear her best dress, her Sunday dress. It was a simple, pale-green cotton dress which she trimmed with a bit of cream lace Olga had given her. Most of the girls in the East End, like Martha, were much too poor to even dream of having a new dress just to get married.

The girls she worked with had other ideas, however, and unbeknown to her, they visited Olga and hatched a plan.

A week before the big day, Martha got a message.

"Martha, I know you're really busy, but could you pop in to see me tonight after you finish work? I really need your help with something."

Martha was surprised. In all the years she had known Olga, the older woman had never asked for any sort of help before. She was fiercely independent and proud, and so Martha was worried. She hurried home that evening, gulped down the cabbage soup and bread her mum had prepared and rushed to the Russian woman's room on the next floor.

As she approached the closed door, she was surprised to hear several voices, laughing and giggling. Olga never had visitors. Occasionally she might have a messenger come from one of the big fashion houses to collect some finished dresses, but apart from that, the little flat was always quiet.

She knocked and waited patiently for Olga or Svetlana to open the door.

"Hello Martha, surprise, surprise!"

The little room was full to bursting, or so it seemed. She blinked, just to be sure she wasn't imagining it.

Everywhere she looked there seemed to be piles of lace, ribbon, and satin.

"What do you think? Do you like it?"

It took her a few minutes to recover her senses. To register that three of the girls who worked with her at Selfridges were standing in the room with huge smiles on their faces.

"Oh Martha, we couldn't wait to show you. It was so hard to keep the secret, especially when you talked about having to get married in your old green dress. We'd already popped in to see Olga and your mum to put together our plan, and as soon as you announced your engagement we got on with it. We've all been pretty busy and between us we've stitched all this for you. We hope you like it."

Martha struggled to keep her tears in check as she looked around the little room.

"We thought we'd make you a whole trousseau. Olga had your measurements, so she cut everything out and then we all took things home to sew in our spare time. It was a bit hard sometimes making sure we could sneak up here without you spotting us!"

One by one they excitedly showed off their handiwork. The lace undergarments, threaded with pale blue ribbon. The cotton nightdresses, trimmed with pretty lace. The handkerchiefs embroidered with her initials and the pale-pink dress, edged with black satin, that would be her "going away outfit."

She suddenly noticed her mum and her sisters crowding 'round by the open front door, big smiles on their faces.

"Oh Mum," she spoke in a very shaky voice and then she burst into tears of joy and happiness. Tears because all these people had shown her how much they loved her, how much she meant to them.

"Okay. Now I think you must wipe away those tears and look at this." Olga spoke with her thick Russian accent and the others gasped as she went behind the curtain that separated the kitchen from the tiny bedroom, returning with something in her arms.

Between them they had all made the most beautiful wedding dress—a frothy concoction of cream satin and lace. It had a small bustle, as was the current fashion, a tiny nipped in waist, and a full skirt draped with yards of fabric. The long sleeves and bodice were edged with fine lace and there were tiny buttons all down the back, covered in the same cream satin.

"We really wanted to use silk, but it was too expensive."

"And of course you'll have to wear a proper corset, but we didn't finish that in time. It will be ready for the wedding, though."

"We did manage to make the veil. Why don't you try it on now?"

The wedding was a joyous affair. As Martha left the house to walk the few hundred steps to the little church, she was bombarded with good wishes. All her neighbours seemed to be lining the cobbled street or hanging out of the tenement windows, hoping to catch a glimpse of the beautiful bride. They were not disappointed.

Wearing her stunning gown, with a coronet of fresh flowers on her head securing the flimsy veil, she looked an absolute picture. In her hand she clasped a little posy of fresh flowers to match her head band. Old George, her dad's cousin, had dropped them off this morning after his shift as a porter at the flower market in Covent Garden.

"A couple of the stallholders wanted to give them to you. They said you always went out of your way to chat with them when you were little. They got some of the flower girls to wire them into a little posy and headdress for you. They sent a buttonhole for Robert, too."

Martha knew the flower girls well. The young girls, many of them her neighbours in the tenement, worked hard for the few shillings they earnt each week. They rose before dawn to get to the flower market at 5:00 a.m., then worked all day peddling their wares on the busy streets. It was a hard life but there was great camaraderie, and some of the women had been selling their violets in the same patch for more than twenty years.

As she approached the old stone church on the arm of her proud father, Martha was overcome with nerves. There were so many people there, people who were thrilled to see one of their own, a girl from the slums, marrying a nice lad. So many girls in the East End were destined to live a life of poverty through no fault of their own. They were born into a life with no opportunity, no chance to step outside the mean streets of the slums. Instead, they would be forced to lead a life full of quiet desperation, sadness, and loss, with nothing much to look forward to from one year to another. They knew they would probably have lots of babies that never lived to become toddlers. They knew that if someone got sick they would probably die, because they couldn't afford a doctor. Some of them, even if they were lucky enough to find a husband, would never know a life of contentment or ease. Others, often very young girls, would be abandoned by the men who impregnated them, they and their children forced into a life of prostitution or in a workhouse.

So today, a wedding was a great cause for celebration. They all cheered heartily as Martha approached the church, and their cheers were even louder an hour later when she emerged as a married woman on the arm of her handsome new husband.

The party afterwards was loud and very jolly. It was something of a shock for Robert's family, who had left their quiet rural life in Hampshire to find themselves experiencing a real Cockney wedding.

But they were good people and they recognised that despite the poverty they saw around them, everyone present was just the same as them. They were all living their lives as best they could, trying to provide for their families.

Robert's parents had not met Martha, their new daughter-in-law, or her family, until the day before the wedding. Robert had written to them telling them all about his bride-to-be, but although they had wanted to be there for the engagement party, they were not able to afford the coach fare twice for the whole family to go to London. So, they had come up the day before the wedding and were all sleeping on the floor in Robert's lodgings.

"Mum, Dad, this is Martha."

Robert had been shy introducing her. He had arranged for everyone to meet in Hyde Park, by the bandstand. He met Martha after work and they strolled up Oxford Street together.

"Oh Robert, will they like me? I do hope your mum does, it will be so awkward otherwise."

He squeezed her hand. Now that they were engaged, it was quite acceptable to hold hands in public. He especially liked it when she took off her kid gloves and he could feel the warmth of her soft hand in his. He even kissed her goodnight now, although they were both shy about kissing if anyone else was around.

"Of course. They'll all love you Martha, I just know they will."

And of course, they did. His mum was thrilled to see him so happy, that he had finally chosen a really nice girl with whom to settle down. His dad thought Martha was wonderful. She was such a pretty girl, with good manners and a kind heart. No wonder his lad had fallen so hard.

The day of the wedding was sunny and warm, and after a few beers and big chunks of wedding cake, the two families had bonded. Everyone was so happy for the young couple, for the bright future full of promises and dreams that stretched before them.

"I just wish you'd move out of this place and come down to the country. It's a much better place to raise a family, lots of fresh air and good food. I don't like to think of my grandchildren growing up in these slums."

"Oh Dad, don't fuss. We like it here. You know I wasn't happy down there. I love the city life, and anyway, I don't think I could ever drag Martha away from her family. She's never known any other kind of life."

The years ticked by, as years always do, and by the time they had been married for eight years, Robert and Martha were parents to seven children. Only five of them had survived. The two youngest, Jack and Edward, had both died when they were just a few months old, snatched away cruelly by disease that was rampant in the overcrowded slums. Martha had been distraught, but had managed to keep going for the sake of her remaining children. It broke her heart to see the pain in Robert's eyes when he came home from work and saw the missing places at the table.

Although they lived in the slums, in rooms on the same floor as Olga, they lived better than most of their neighbours. Robert's job at the printers was secure, albeit not very well paid, but there was just enough to scrape by every week. Martha had been forced to give up her job at Selfridges after the wedding, as married women were not considered suitable employees. At the time, she hadn't minded too much, she had been so happy making her new little home and the babies started coming pretty much straight away. Their first, little Robert, had been born exactly ten months after their wedding, with the others following in quick succession. Now she only had little Valentine under her feet all day; the others were all at school. They went to a ragged school, a place for poor children to get an education. Here they learnt reading, writing, and arithmetic, and there was great emphasis on the Bible. Martha was glad; she wanted her children to learn so they could have a chance to make something of themselves. Her time working in Oxford Street made her realise that a big, exciting world existed out there. Though it was a world she was likely never to see, perhaps one day her children could.

Just before his fifth birthday, Valentine George and his family went to the country. It was the first time he and his brothers and sisters had ever left London. His mum had never been out of the city either, never left the dirt and grime of the busy streets to exchange them for wide open spaces and green fields as far as the eye could see. They travelled to Hampshire by carriage–well, wagon really–their mode of transport was certainly not anything as posh as the smart carriages that overtook them on the long and uncomfortable journey. They didn't care either way, to the kids, it was a real adventure.

Robert smiled as he watched the excited faces of his children. They were city children, born and raised within the sound of the Bow Bells, proper little Cockneys. In fact, little Rose, his only and most precious daughter, had just one ambition, to become a Pearly Queen. She was a rather dramatic little girl, probably as the result of being the only girl in the family and therefore spoilt by the rest of them. They often joked that she would go on stage one day and they would all get free tickets to watch her perform at the music hall. At nine years old, little Rose knew, absolutely knew, that one day she would be famous. Becoming a Pearly Queen, in her eyes, was a very good start. Both her parents had tried to explain to her that it wasn't possible, that she didn't come from a long line of costermongers, so therefore she was not eligible to be a pearlie. They tried to tell her how lucky she was to go to school, to have the chance to get an education, but little Rose would not be shifted. She wanted to wear clothes covered in pearl buttons and spend all her days not at some boring school, but instead being a flower girl, selling bunches of violets or snowdrops to passing toffs in the street.

None of the boys had such ambitions. They were just content being boys, playing in the cobbled streets with their mates and tolerating school because their dad said they had to, all the while desperate to grow up and get jobs that would pay a few shillings. None of them dreamt of much more, although sometimes Robert junior had a faraway look in his eyes that his mum knew meant he was thinking of other places, places he read about in the newspaper. His dad brought a newspaper home every night. He got a free copy from the office where he worked, and once he had read it from cover to cover he laid it aside and his eldest son would pick it up and sit on the floor, engrossed in what he was reading.

On any given night, a fly on their wall might hear, "Mum, what does 'Boer' mean?"

Martha would look up from the stove where she was stirring a cabbage stew.

"Sorry love. I don't know what you're talking about."

"It says here that the Second Boer War is very bloody and that soldiers from all over the Empire are going there to fight."

"Oh love, just ask your dad. He understands these things much better than I do."

In truth Martha always understood very well, but she was a woman of her generation, brought up to act as though men were somehow the superior sex and should be deferred to at all times. In her heart, she knew this wasn't true. She had spent her whole life watching men–her father, brothers, uncles, and neighbours. Good men mostly, although there was the odd wife beater or drunkard amongst them. They all had a vague air of superiority, that feeling instilled in them from the day they were born that told them they were the possessors of not just more physical strength, but also greater intellect and understanding of the world, as compared to a mere woman. Martha, however, had been around enough women to be of the opinion that in fact, *they* were the stronger sex. After all, men didn't have to cope with pregnancy or childbirth! She admired those taking part in the Suffrage movement hugely, that brave band of women fighting so hard for equal rights. Even though Martha knew in her heart that the inferiority assigned to women was unjust, she could not bear to change the ways of her upbringing in her own home.

"Look Dad. Just look at all those fields! They go on for miles and miles and miles. I bet if you started walking over them, you'd never reach the end. I bet they go on right to the edge of the world."

Robert smiled at John, his second-born son. John was a quiet boy, kind and thoughtful in equal measures. Everyone loved him.

"Don't be daft, John. You have to get to the sea before you reach the edge of the world. The English Channel. And then you get to France."

Robert junior, who was almost eleven years old, was an expert on everything. He was a nice-enough boy, but he took great delight in teasing his younger siblings, constantly reminding them that he had been going to school much longer, and therefore knew more than they did. There was no malice in his teasing; he was just utterly sure that he was superior.

"I just love all the cows and sheep. Will there be any at Granddad's farm?"

They were on their way to Alton, to stay in the old farmhouse where Robert had grown up. The house he had lived in until he was 17, deciding then to move to London and make his fortune.

He hadn't made any fortune, of course, but he had met his Martha. The love of her and their children were, to him, riches beyond measure.

"Yes, my love, there are lots of cows, sheep, chickens, and pigs on the farm. You'll have a wonderful time and I expect, if you're really good, Granddad and Granny will even let you help feed them every day."

The two-week holiday they had planned passed quickly. Robert's parents were delighted to meet their grandchildren for the first time, and very happy days were had by all. The children lost their grey pallor and filled out due to all the home cooking. Their grandma spoilt them with cakes, pies, and biscuits, and at every meal the table was groaning with home-killed meat, vegetables from the garden, and crusty, freshly-baked bread. For children used to simple, but rather poor fare, it was all a huge luxury. None of them really looked forward to returning to London.

The night before Robert, Martha, and the kids were due to leave, Robert's father had a massive heart attack. By the next morning, he was gone. He was just 53 years old. Robert's mother was bereft, clinging to her son as if he were her only hope of survival. The days turned into weeks and the weeks into months and still she clung to him, weeping every time he talked about returning to London. In the end he sent a message to his employer, begging for an extended absence of leave. The farm was beginning to suffer from neglect. He was no farmer and had never wanted to be, but he owed it to his mother to try and keep it going. His family had been tenant farmers there for the last 200 years, and although he didn't want to inherit it, it was likely that one of his sons or nephews would be interested in doing so.

So they stayed. The children attended the little village school and thrived. They all enjoyed the fresh air, the good food, and the more relaxed lifestyle. After a while, Robert even found himself enjoying working on the farm. Every evening after dinner, his mother would play the piano and they would all sit around the big farmhouse table drinking cups of tea. Sometimes they would dance, Martha teaching her children, each one in turn, how to waltz. "One, two, three, one, two, three."

One day, after they had been there for about six months, there was a terrible accident.

"Mum, Mum, come now. Dad's fallen over and he won't get up."

Martha rushed out to the field nearest the house. They called it the First Field, presumably because it was the first one you saw from the kitchen window. Robert was lying there barely moving, his face drooping. At once, she knew it was a stroke. She had seen her grandfather like that, just before he died.

Robert, the love of her life and father to her five living children, was buried in the little church graveyard at the age of just 32. He was laid to rest in the county of his birth and never to return to London, the place he had chosen to call home.

Martha and the children were grief-stricken. It had all happened so suddenly, the entire last half year, really. Robert had been snatched away from his family with no warning and now, here they were, stuck in a country village on a farm miles from everything they knew and held dear.

"I think it's time you lot went back where you came from. Sadie and I are going to move back here to take care of Mum. It's what Dad would have wanted."

Robert's elder brother, Sam, had turned up for the funeral with his wife and four children in tow. They had been living in Portsmouth, a seaside town some 25 miles away, so it made sense that they had stayed over at the farm after the funeral rather than rushing back to town. Sam worked at the naval base as a docker. He was a big, rough man, very different from Martha's gentle husband. Robert had been so kind and considerate, always putting the needs of others before himself, but his brother was a different kettle of fish altogether. He drank too much, shouted constantly at his wife and children, and treated his mother as if she was his servant. But like mothers the world over, Robert's mother could see no fault in "her boy." When he suggested that "Perhaps, now that Dad's gone, I should move back here to the farm, to run it and take care of everything for you," she happily agreed. She was thrilled at the prospect of having at least one of her precious boys back under her roof. Just one week after the funeral, Robert's widow and five young children left the comfort of the family farmhouse and returned to life in London—a life of drudgery and hardship.

THE EAST END OF LONDON
1913

Martha tightened her shawl around her shoulders. It was a flimsy thing, well-worn and not really capable of keeping out the cold wind, but it was the best she had–the only one not full of holes. She was in a hurry to get home; the boys would be back from work any minute now and she couldn't trust Rose to get their dinner on the table in time. That was, if she even remembered she was supposed to be cooking at all!

Rose, her only daughter. She was a lovely girl, but not really domesticated. In fact, not at all domesticated, quite the opposite. She was something else.. Martha smiled to herself as she thought about her beloved girl. Rose was nothing like most of the other young ladies in the East End. She was not content with the idea of being "just a wife and mother." No, her girl wanted more, much more. Martha was thrilled about that. She was so hopeful for Rose, excited that her girl was going to have a better life than she had had. She just knew her daughter would have more chances, more opportunities to fulfill her wildest dreams.

Martha then thought about her own life as she hurriedly made her way back to her home. This was a life she had been forced to live, one that began when she became a newly-widowed mother of five children, all five under the age of eleven. Thank goodness they had been well-behaved, or she would not have known what to do. Luckily, none of them had ever really given her a moment's trouble–until now.

"I don't understand why you're making such a fuss, Mum."

"Oh son," She had struggled to keep her tears in check. The others sat around the old kitchen table with their gaping mouths, hardly believing what their eldest brother was saying.

"You know I've always hated London. I loved it in the country. If Dad was still alive, I probably wouldn't be going, but he isn't and I want to make something of my life, not just fester here doing a job I hate and marrying some simple-minded girl I can't have a decent conversation with."

"How dare you call girls simple minded? Maybe it's *you* that's the problem, Robert. Maybe girls just don't find you interesting enough to talk to!"

Rose hated it when any of her brothers said anything derogatory about women. She was an avid feminist and especially supported the suffragettes.

"You just want to run away 'cos you can't get a girlfriend. All the nice ones like our Valentine best. They even prefer our John to you. At least he's polite and nice to them; he doesn't just take advantage of one and move on to the next."

It was true. Robert junior was a very good-looking young man, the spitting image of his late father. Sadly though, he didn't have his father's gentle nature. He wasn't really a family person either; his younger brothers irritated him and he found his feisty sister too much to bear. He loved his mother Martha, but treated her rather badly, almost as though she were his personal servant.

"Oh shut up you lot, you don't know what you're talking about."

"But son, why do you have to go so far away? I'm sure you could go down to Hampshire instead and get a nice job there," Martha tried to reason. "You liked it there, remember? You have always said you wished we'd never come back to London."

Robert stood up, irritated by everyone's arguments.

"Well, it's too late to change my mind now. I've got a passage booked on a ship leaving for Africa next week. None of you can make me stay."

With that, he stomped out of the room, slamming the door behind him. They could hear his footsteps clomping down the wooden staircase and the thump of the heavy front door closing as he left the building.

Martha burst into tears, sobbing loudly and wiping her wet face with the edges of her old shawl.

"Oh Mum, don't worry. We're all here to take care of you. He was never at home much anyway."

It was true. Robert junior had always chosen to spend most of his free time away from the family home, but honestly, who could blame him?

When they had returned to London after Robert's sudden death they had been forced to move into different lodgings, as their old place had already been rented out to another family. The new place was worse. It was close, in another tenement building just off Commercial Road, but it was much more dilapidated. It existed in a dark, gloomy passage with no running water or toilet inside–just a shared tap in the courtyard. While they were grateful for the shelter, Martha still struggled to make enough money to pay the rent that their greedy landlord demanded every week.

It had been so hard for her at first. She was in shock, utterly traumatised at losing her beloved husband. She was barely able to function and struggled to cope with the demands of raising her children. In the beginning they had stayed with her family, all squashed into two small rooms with her parents and the three siblings who still lived at home. With their loving help she got through the first couple of weeks, the truly dark days of her grief. Given the choice she would have stayed there forever, comforted by the loving arms of her family. The world had other plans, though. When the landlord found out about the extra tenants, he threatened them *all* with eviction. Martha didn't want her parents to lose their home; and it was the only home she had known growing up. Her mother and father had been through so much already, and they were now in trouble because they tried to help her. The dock strike back in 1889 had been such a dreadful time for her parents and so many others in the East End. If it hadn't been for the kindness of the people at the East London Methodist Mission, many of them would have died of starvation. The good people there had set up a soup kitchen named the Mahogany Bar and had fed a thousand meals a day to the starving dockers and their families.

Knowing she couldn't continue to put her parents in jeopardy of losing their home, Martha had found the new rooms with Olga's help. They were hideous, damp, and vermin riddled, but at least they provided a roof over the heads of her and her children, a home of sorts for their family's new start.

Olga was a great support through it all, as she had always been. In truth, she was delighted to have Martha back in London; she had missed her terribly when they went off to the country. Svetlana was a wonderful help with the kids, always happy to watch them if Martha needed to go out or was too busy to keep a careful eye on them. All the children had therefore grown up knowing and loving Svetlana, not frightened by her occasional epileptic fits as others were. Instead, they just learnt to make sure she was in a safe position, then they would stand by, watching carefully until her body stopped convulsing and she was able to get up again.

Despite their worsening poverty, once their raw grief had worn off a little, they did find some happiness again. They were all together, they had a roof over their heads, and somehow, Martha managed to scrape together enough pennies every day to feed them properly. Sometimes it was just gruel or watery stew with stale bread, but there was always love and laughter at their table. The children returned to the ragged school they had attended before going to the country. Then, the older boys left when they were able, finding jobs to support the household.

Robert junior had been delighted to leave school at the age of twelve to become a newspaper hawker. He would roam the streets selling papers–often having to fight with other boys to claim his "patch"–but he loved the life. One of his favorite memories was of reading the papers his dad brought home from work in the evenings, in those seemingly far-off days when his dad was still alive. He loved to read about news from around the world, there were so many people and places thousands of miles away. He was intent on visiting them all someday.

Now, years later, here he was, announcing to his family that he was going to Africa to follow his dreams.

"Oh son, whatever will we do without you? Will I ever see you again? Africa is so very far away."

In truth, Martha had no idea where Africa was. She just knew it was somewhere thousands of miles away, a place that was going to swallow her precious boy up.

"Mum, I can't stay here. This place just isn't enough for me. I hate the dirt and the grime. I hate the crowded alleys and the poverty. I just want a life where I can be free–free to enjoy wide open spaces, free to hold my face up to the sunshine, free to live a better life."

A week later, he was gone. He left to seek his fortune in a land far, far away. He told his brothers of his plans to get rich by finding gold or diamonds and to see wild animals–elephants, lions, tigers–in their natural habitat. In typical Robert fashion, he made sure to remind his siblings they would only ever see creatures like these in the zoo, while he intended to see them in all the glory of their homeland.

His plans were so glorious, were told with such enthusiasm, that his younger brothers began to think that maybe they should be brave enough to follow him in a year or two, once he was properly settled. Martha's young sons had no way of knowing that the world had other plans for them.

John was a year younger than Robert and of a totally different character. He was a very thoughtful boy, both quiet and gentle. From a very young age, and certainly since their father died, he had felt it was his place to take care of his mother, sister, and younger brothers. He rarely thought of his own needs, always putting everyone else first. He too had left school when he was twelve years old to become an errand boy, getting work wherever he could. Sometimes he ran errands for the local market traders, sometimes the local match factory employed him, occasionally he was asked to deliver messages to the local midwives. His favourite jobs were when he was sent to the docks or Covent Garden or Billingsgate Market, because the porters would feel sorry for him and slip a bit of meat, fish, or bread his way. He would take these precious items straight home. After he proudly placed the food on the kitchen table, his mum would pat him on the head and tell him what a wonderful son he was. She would remark how because of him, she would "eat like the Queen herself tonight."

These were some of John's happiest moments—moments that kept him going when he was running around the dirty streets with holes in his shoes and clothes that were nowhere near warm enough to shield him from the biting winds that came from the river. He loved the River Thames and the East

End, and he didn't care about the hardships he had to encounter if it meant he could help his mum and siblings. He absolutely loved his family.

Albert, the next youngest, was the artist of the family. He was a good-looking little boy who turned into an incredibly attractive young man. By the age of 14 he was earning his living drawing portraits.

At first he had just done them for his neighbours, charging them nothing, just excited to use his talent and to make people happy. If a new baby was born or someone got married, he would give the family a beautifully-executed drawing to mark the occasion.

One day, just before he left school for good at the same age of his brothers, he had been sitting on the pavement outside the George and Dragon Pub on Commercial Road, sketching in the street, something happened. He often sat there or outside some of the other pubs nearby with no outstanding event, simply fascinated by the men and women who frequented the places. He was interested in their stories, their tales of life. Many of these people were dockers or porters from the local markets, and their faces were lined with years of hard work and worry. Each person's face carried so much character, and they were all wonderful subjects to draw.

He always had a ready supply of paper and pencils. One of the teachers at his school, Miss Jane Percival, a wealthy young woman from Mayfair who volunteered at the school three days a week, had recognised Albert's outstanding talent and kept him constantly supplied with the tools he needed.

"I say, lad. You're pretty talented. Where did you learn to draw like that?"

On this day, a man approached him. This man was a stranger, not someone Albert had ever seen before. He had just come out of the tobacconist's shop that was next door to the pub.

"You could make a pretty penny selling your drawings up West. All those toffs and their ladies would pay you handsomely to make their likenesses, I reckon."

At school the next day, after the bell had rung, signalling the end of the school day, the young boy lingered behind.

"Miss Percival?"

"Yes, Albert?"

"Please, Miss, I was just wondering if you thought I'd be good enough to earn a living doing my drawings. It'd be nice to do that instead of working down the docks or at the match factory."

The young woman's heart went out to the thin, pale boy standing before her. She had recognised his amazing talent years ago, when he was just nine years old. She also knew that it would almost certainly be wasted, it would never be realised if he lived the rest of his life just surviving in the slums, eking out a living to help his widowed mother. It was so unfair. If only he had been born into a different life, a life like hers, full of wealth and opportunity. His talent would have been noticed and encouraged. He would have ended up going to university or art school, completing his education by being sent on a Grand Tour and visiting all the capitals of Europe to study the paintings of the Old Masters. Instead, he was destined for a life of poverty and obscurity, forced to exhaust his talents just to survive.

At times like this, Jane Percival hated being a woman. She was a woman who had been born into a life of luxury, yes, but had absolutely no means of her own. She would always be answerable to either her father or a husband, never having money of her own that she could spend as she saw fit. It made her blood boil. How she wished she could help this little lad. If she had been in charge of her own destiny she would whisk him away from the slums right now to give him the kind of life he deserved, a life full of opportunity. That was why she supported the suffragettes. They were all brave women fighting for equality, for the chance that all women could have a say, could have their rights, the same as any man.

The best Jane could do for this lad was keep him supplied with paper and pencils. She could not manage to do more; she couldn't give him the opportunity he deserved. She had to fight hard enough to be allowed to work at this school. Her father had been horrified that his only daughter had wanted to volunteer at such an establishment, to be exposed to all the horrors of the working-class area. They had argued about it for months. He had been very reluctant to let his beautiful daughter work at all; why could she not be like all the other young women of her class? Why couldn't she be content with just sitting at home, doing a bit of embroidery or reading a few novels? Better yet, why could she not want to spend her time planning what to wear to the next social event, where she might ensnare a rich husband? He certainly didn't want his precious girl going into the slums of the East End every day;

everyone knew they were full of unspeakable diseases, dens of vice and decay..

In the end, obviously, he had weakened, but only because Jane kept threatening to join the suffragette movement, to become one of those strident women who chained themselves to the railings at Parliament and other such nonsense. So instead of becoming a subject of ridicule–many fathers and brothers of those women were ridiculed because they were clearly not capable of keeping their womenfolk in check–he reluctantly agreed that she could travel to the ragged school in Stepney. There were conditions though: she was allowed to go only three days a week, and always in the company of her maid, Alice, and their coach driver, Tom.

Jane Percival, despite her gilded life, had a heart of gold. It distressed her greatly to see how the people of the East End suffered simply because of the accident of birth. This accident saw them born into poverty and despair, a life of unimaginable hardship and suffering. In all the years she had worked at the school, she had never become accustomed to the sight and smells of the young people in her care. The building was filled with small children who were often emaciated, covered in bruises and scars. The bruises were many times fresh, acquired after a heavy night's drinking by their father. These kids often had head lice or sores. Their clothes, although mostly clean, were old and ill fitting, having been passed down from older brothers and sisters. While a few of the students were better dressed–clean pinafores with white aprons, shiny ribbons in their well-brushed hair–these were few and far between. Yet, what was most amazing was that they still managed to find joy in their lives. For example, they made their own toys from scraps of wood. The girls brought their treasured dolls to school with them—much-loved playthings made from old wooden washing pegs with charcoal faces drawn on and makeshift dresses fashioned from scraps of old discarded material. The utter unfairness of it all just broke Jane's heart. She thought about her cousins, little girls of much the same age but from wealthy families. These girls played once or twice with expensive china dolls—the ones with shiny golden locks and the best silk and satin dresses—before discarding them as soon as the next gift arrived.

LONDON
SEPTEMBER 1914

Martha felt as though her heart was about to break. She had already lost two sons for good, lost them before they even had a chance to grow into toddlers. Another had been lost by way of wandering across continents. Now, she was going to lose her last three beloved boys to the bloodshed of the war.

"Oh Mum, don't cry. We'll be back before you know it."

"He's right, Mum. They reckon it'll all be over by Christmas. You'll hardly have any time to miss us."

"And Lily Rose says she's happy to move in here with you and Rose if you like. It's a bit crowded in Stanhope Street, and if she comes here you can both help her when the baby arrives."

Since Robert had gone off to seek his fortune in Africa, the house had been much calmer.

John was still an errand boy, but he was so popular with all the market traders these days that he brought home treats almost every night: a shuck of oysters, a rabbit, a big basket of fruit and veg that wouldn't last 'till the market opened the next day. They had never eaten so well.

Albert was making good money with his portrait drawing. He had become quite well known and he now sat sketching on the steps of St Paul's, or sometimes Piccadilly Circus below the statue of Eros, his tweed cap on the pavement full of coins from admiring passers-by.

As for Valentine, well, his life had changed beyond all measure in the last year. He now had a wife, and a baby on the way.

He never was too excited about school. Once he could read and write, he lost interest. Valentine hated reciting his times tables, a chore that his teachers set every day.

6 x 4 = 24

7 x 4 = 28

8 x 4 = 32

It was such a waste of time; he wanted to be out in the real world, making his way in life like his brothers were. He already had the promise of a job when he left school. Since he was a little lad he had loved horses and had always been willing to hold their reins while their owners went about their business. Sometimes they slipped him a few pennies for his trouble, other times they just thanked him and told him to get on his way. By the time he was ready to leave school he had established his reputation as a reliable and willing boy–one to trust. He soon had a regular clientele, traders who needed a lad to look after their horse and cart while they bargained their wares. He began to bring home a few shillings every week and the little family thrived.

Martha was still sewing with Olga, making dresses for the rich and famous. Just lately they had been making some stage costumes for the famous music hall performer, Vesta Tilley.

"Oh by the way, Mum, have you heard Miss Tilley's new song? They were playing it down at the recruiting office when we were all queuing up there today. It's really good, it's called, *"We Don't Want to Lose You, but We Think You 'Ought to Go."*

Martha stopped sobbing for a moment and smiled ruefully. She had so enjoyed making stage clothes for Vesta, it had been such fun to go to see her perform. She was seen wearing the beautiful dresses that Martha and Olga had laboured over for so long, then she also appeared on stage dressed as a man. Martha remembered that the two of them had been a bit shocked. She impersonated a variety of male characters: a judge, a policeman, and an upper-class idle toff known as "Burlington Bertie." But her boyish swagger and comical skits and songs had brought the house down. Now it seemed she was dressing as a soldier, enticing boys like Martha's to join the army, to fight for King and Country.

"Oh Valentine, what ever does your Lily say? She must be heartbroken that you've joined up, especially when you've got a little one on the way?"

"She's all right, Mum. She wasn't very happy when I told her, though. She cried a lot, just like you're doing now. But John is right, it probably will be all over by Christmas. I don't suppose we'll even get the chance to do any fighting."

Martha looked at her three sons. Her beautiful boys, the apples of her eye. They were so young, so bright eyed and bushy tailed, so sure that it was all going to be a wonderful adventure, that they would be home again by Christmas.

She sank into the old wooden chair by the fire and wrapped her shawl tightly around her. It was a new one; the boys had clubbed together last Christmas to buy it for her. It was red and very soft, made from lamb's wool. Until now it had been her most-treasured possession, but suddenly as she looked down at it, all she could see was red blood. Blood from all the young men, young men like her precious boys, who would undoubtedly be killed during this horrible, unnecessary war.

She had been so happy just six months ago. Her children were thriving, all working hard and bringing home enough money so they could all live a bit more comfortably. She missed Robert junior of course, worried about him constantly out there in that big continent called Africa. She often wondered if she would ever see him again or if he was lost to her forever. But overall, she found joy in her life with her children and their little home.

Rose was now working as a waitress at Lyons Corner House in the Strand and the work suited her very well. She started her career at the original branch of Lyons at 123 Piccadilly, but when they opened their flagship store in Coventry Street in 1909 she had transferred there, enjoying the hustle and bustle of the huge new establishment. She loved the grand atmosphere, the enormous dining halls with their marble pillars, starched white linen tablecloths, and the smart uniform she wore. Naturally pretty and rather flirtatious, she charmed the male customers and her fellow workers alike.

Her life seemed to be a constant round of outings and parties, and she was never short of male admirers.

Martha admired her daughter greatly. Rose was living exactly the kind of life she would have loved to live herself: a life of fun, music, dancing, and laughter. None of the young men who courted her were quite right, though. She had very high standards and although most of them were lovely chaps, real gentlemen who never tried to take advantage of her, she was still waiting. Waiting to find her Mr. Right. In the meantime, until he turned up on her doorstep, she was determined to have a bit of fun. She was a very snappy dresser too, always wearing the latest fashions. Lately she had taken to wearing a beret perched jauntily on top of her brunette curls. She got a job lot of them down at the market in Petticoat Lane in every colour imaginable. They weren't even fashionable when she bought them, but somehow she had become a trendsetter. Before too long, lots of the other girls were wearing berets too, although, in Martha's opinion, they didn't look half as elegant as her girl!

Martha looked lovingly at her daughter. Rose had her head down on the old kitchen table. Her shoulders were shaking and her tears were dripping onto the embroidered white cloth.

"But why did you all have to sign up so soon? Couldn't you have waited a bit? Waited 'till the worst was over? You might be my horrible brothers, but I don't want to lose you."

Rose had seen plenty of tears over the last few weeks. So many young men like her brothers had signed up without really knowing what they were signing up for. They were all falling for the propaganda being put out by the War Office. Fighting for King and Country indeed.

"Well, it's too late now. We've done it and that's that. Now we just have to wait and find out where they're sending us. Hopefully we can all go together. I've always wanted to go to France."

"Oh Valentine, please don't go. How am I ever going to cope without you? This baby and I need you *here*, not off in some foreign land. You aren't even a fighter, you hate hurting anything. You won't even squash a fly."

Valentine looked at his wife and smiled sadly. She was right. He wasn't really a fighter, but now he had no choice. He had signed up voluntarily, had heeded the call for all fit young men to defend their homeland. Now here he was in scratchy khaki green, saying goodbye to his beloved Lily and not knowing if he would ever see her again. Not knowing if he would ever hold his unborn child in his arms.

It had all seemed like such an adventure at first—a respite from his rather dull existence. A break from hard work and relentless poverty. A chance to do something different, to see the world, to see how other people lived. Now it was really happening though, now he was standing in his mum's kitchen and saying goodbye to all the people he loved most in the world. Now it didn't seem like an adventure at all.

Just a few short months ago, life had been so simple. He had met and married the girl of his dreams and then found out he was going to be a father. It seemed like it was so long ago, the day he stood in the little stone church and watched his Lily walk down the aisle toward him.

LILY ROSE SCARBOROUGH
1914

Lily Rose Scarborough was just nineteen years old when she married Valentine George, the love of her life. She had only known him for a few months, but she knew, absolutely knew, he was the one.

The day she met him for the first time, she had been to visit her Aunty Mabel, who lived in a tiny cottage alongside the Regent's Canal. Aunty Mabel was her mum's youngest sister, a very pretty lady who had married well, stepped outside her life in the slums, and married a cabinet maker. He earnt a good living and could therefore provide his wife and children with a decent home. Lily loved going to visit. Although it was only a two-up, two-down, old brick house, to the young girl it seemed like a mansion. They had a proper parlour adjoining the kitchen, and upstairs there were two small bedrooms. There was no bathroom or inside toilet, but they did have a privy in the little concrete yard with an outside tap which they only had to share with one other neighbour. To Lily, who had always lived in the crowded tenement in Stanhope Street with her mum, dad, and three brothers, it seemed like heaven.

"Lily love, do you mind popping to Aunty Mabel's this morning? She's promised to lend me a few quid to help with the expenses."

Lily raised her eyebrows. She hated that her mum was always asking people for money. She found it really embarrassing, especially when she knew it would just be wasted on snuff or gin.

"Oh Mum, do I have to? Can't you send one of the boys instead?"

"No love, I can't. None of them are talking to me at the minute."

Lily sighed. She knew exactly why her brothers had fallen out with their mum. It happened every single week. Without fail.

"Oh Mum, why do you keep doing it? I just don't understand why you always behave like this."

"Now listen here, my girl. If you had the life I have to suffer, you'd take snuff and drink gin too. It's my only pleasure, my only comfort."

Lily pulled a face, but didn't respond. They had had this discussion so many times and it always ended the same. *She* would be the one who had to go begging to her aunt. Her mum, who was the cause of all the drama, would never go, mostly because she knew what her sister would say. How she would lecture her about living a better life, coming to terms with her reality, not always trying to mask her existence with snuff and alcohol. How she would be told she was ruining her children's lives, driving them away with her bad habits and selfish behaviour.

"Well, you'd better get going quick, young lady. The boys will be home from work soon and you know what that means."

Lily knew exactly what it meant. Her three big brothers: Tom, Dick, and Harry would all come home from work tired and hungry, and would be greeted by their mother in a state of stupor, slumped in front of the dying fire, no food on the table. No delicious hot dinners for them, not unless she trudged all the way over to the house on Regent's Canal and got some cash from their aunty.

She was tired when she eventually got back to Stanhope Street. It was a long walk from there to her aunt's house, and although she had received a warm welcome, a cup of hot tea, and a chunk of fresh bread thickly spread with butter, she had been uncomfortable. She loved her Aunty Mabel and hated having to ask her for help.

"Aunty Mabel? Mum said you might be able to help her a bit. You know, with a few shillings."

The older woman sighed deeply and fished into her purse, opening the cheap, gold-coloured clasp on the pretty green tapestry bag which was embroidered with pink and purple flowers. The purse was her pride and joy, her husband had given it to her the previous Christmas. She took out a few coins and put them gently into the girl's hand.

"Oh Lily, love. I hate that she makes you do this, sends you on her errands. It just isn't fair. If you were my daughter I would never put you through such things. Sometimes I am ashamed to call her my sister. At first I thought it was your dad dying that sent her like this, just her grief making her behave so badly. But it's been five years now, and I think she's getting worse. The last time I came to your place I couldn't believe how bad she'd got. I do worry about you, lass. The boys are big and ugly enough to cope, but you shouldn't have to live like that."

It was true. Her mum was getting worse. Lily just wished she could live with her Aunty Mabel. How wonderful it would be to live there all the time, in that lovely house, where everyone was calm and quiet.

Sarah Scarborough, Lily's mum, was a broken soul. When her husband was alive she had been an attractive vibrant woman, certain of her place in the world. She was loved by and loving to her husband and children. But after her husband died, having been killed in a street brawl after a boozy night at the pub, she had quickly gone into a decline. She began to neglect her home. She rarely washed or combed her once-beautiful hair. She seemed to forget she had four wonderful and growing children who lost their father. She began to drink. Just a snifter here or there, then more regularly, until every afternoon she was found in a drunken daze in the kitchen, her long, greasy, unwashed hair lying across the table. The same table where, if there had been any food in the house, it would have been served. But there was no food.

"For God's sake, Ma. What do you do with all the money? We give you our wages every week, all three of us, and yet there's never any food to come home to."

It had taken them all a while to realise that she was drinking every day to drown her sorrows.

At first they had been sympathetic. They loved her and they all knew how much she had adored their dad. Even though he had beaten her occasionally–when he had spent a bit too long in the pub–she always forgave him and worshipped the very ground on which he walked. Her own reason for living left the earth when he did. And five years later, it was just getting worse. Her children's patience was beginning to wear thin.

"Ma, do you really have to do this every single week? It's not a joke anymore, you're ruining our lives. Why can't you be normal–a normal mum like our mates have? Dad would be so ashamed to see you like this."

"Oh boys, I'm sorry. The money just kind of ran out. I've sent our Lily over to your Aunty Mabel's to borrow some. She should be back soon."

"We haven't even had any dinner and now we've got to go out again because of you."

"We're sick of it Mum, really sick of it. We work so hard all week and you can't even be bothered to make dinner or wash the clothes, and this place is a pigsty." "Why do you do this to us?"

When Sarah had first started drinking shortly after her husband's untimely death, the housekeeping money had managed to stretch enough to buy some food and a few bottles of gin. But, as her craving for the "Mother's ruin" took hold, she found herself spending less on food for her family and more (and more) on the demon drink. To try and stop her cravings she started taking snuff, an unpleasant and very unladylike habit she had seen her old grandmother do and had always vowed never to do herself. Things had changed though, and addiction had won. Now here she was, in a permanent state of escape.

It was Friday–the last day of the working week–a day they all looked forward to. A whole weekend stretched before them, time for freedom, time to spend the hours with their mates and their sweethearts. And what had their mum done? Again. "Now, like always, we've got to go and see that old devil to get our suits back. It just isn't fair."

Every Monday morning for the last few months, their mother had collected up their suits. One suit each, the only decent piece of clothing any of them owned. Their Sunday best. The boys saved up so long and hard to buy these clothes, putting aside a few coppers each week until they each had enough to visit the old Jewish tailor in Brick Lane and buy a second-hand suit, one that some wealthy gent had cast aside when he had a new one made. Second-hand the suits may have been, but Tom, Dick, and Harry were very proud of them. They were proud of how smart they looked every Friday night as they set out, all clean and brushed up ready for their night out.

"Why do you have to do this, Mum? Don't you love us at all? If Dad was still here, he'd be so angry."

Every Monday for the last few months, their mother had collected their suits from the old wooden wardrobe in the room they all shared and took them to the pawn shop. She exchanged them all for a few shillings to buy more of her beloved gin and snuff.

"Oh don't go on so, boys. All you have to do is go down there with these tickets and you can get them back. It won't cost you much. I did a good deal, told the old man you'd be in as usual."

And so, every week, the young men had to trudge to the old pawn shop on the high street and hand over some of their hard-earned cash to buy back their own suits, knowing that it would all happen again the following week. Week in, week out, until their mother either came to her senses or dropped dead.

As Lily strolled back home, dawdling alongside the canal in no hurry to get back to the unpleasant atmosphere or the totally justified anger of her brothers, she met *him*. A tall, thin young man with twinkly bright blue eyes. He tipped his hat at her as she passed and she smiled shyly. Her smile must have made him brave, for he stopped in his tracks and spoke to her.

"Hello. I don't think I've seen you along here before, have I?"

"No. I don't often come this way, I've been visiting my aunty. She lives just up there, in one of those old houses."

"Oh, so you don't live around here?"

"No, I live in Camden. Stanhope Street. Do you know it?"

She realised she was talking too much. Certainly she would never usually talk like this, not even to people she knew. She was quite shy, really. But somehow he didn't seem like a stranger, more like an old friend.

"Oh yes, I know Stanhope Street. I've got a mate there, lives at number 97 I think."

After that, their budding relationship only catapulted. He *happened* to bump into her the next Saturday when she went to the market. He *happened* to be visiting his friend one day as she was walking home from work. Then he got brave and asked her out for a walk. They walked to Regent's Park and as they strolled she found herself telling him about her life, how she had wanted to train as a seamstress but her mother had stopped her. How she had told her she needed to stay at home and not have such silly notions. Her dad had been happy for her to follow her dreams, but when he had died she had to find a job–any job–just to contribute to the family income. She ended up as a drudge, working in a garment factory off Old Kent Road, running errands and sweeping up all the discarded bits of fabric. She watched with envy as the other women sat at their industrial machines sewing garments. If only she could have been one of them.

Valentine George listened to her story and felt like crying. She was so pretty and brave. All his protective male instincts arose and he vowed to himself, there and then, that one day he would make this beautiful young woman his wife and he would treat her like a princess.

And so he did. Just six months after their first meeting they were married. Now she was expecting his baby, and he was going off to war.

THE WAR YEARS
1914-1918

Travelling from the East End of London to Egypt was a difficult transition for Valentine George.

He had never before been out of reach of his close-knit family. Never left the cobbled streets of the city, full of horse-drawn carts and double-decker buses and vans all emblazoned with advertising slogans: **BOVRIL, NESTLE'S MILK, PEARS SOAP, ZEBRA PLATE POLISH.** He had never *not* had the comforting sound of the Bow Bells to time his day. He had never *not* had the sight and smell of the River Thames–*his* river–wrangling his senses. That was all changing now.

At the train station wearing their brand-new khaki uniforms, all the young men had felt excited. Some of them had never owned new clothes before; all their lives, they had worn hand-me-downs and used second-hand things that had been on many bodies before theirs. By going off to war, they were leaving behind their life of drudgery, of servitude. They were giving up their spots working in poorly-paid jobs at factories, warehouses, and in service. Going off to fight in this war and protect King and Country was an adventure. When it was all over, these men were going to return to a different, better world.

Egypt 1914

My Darling Lily,

How I miss you. It seems like forever since I held you in my arms. I can't believe I am now a father. I bet little Henry looks just like you, sweet and beautiful. Don't want him taking after his ugly old dad!

Seriously my darling, I do hope you and baby are keeping well. I'm not sure if you will get this letter, the old censors seem to be doing a good job at keeping most stuff secret; I guess they think we Tommies will tell our sweethearts too much. So I'm not really expecting this to arrive in Camden Town, but I just want you to know that I love you, miss you all terribly, and can't wait for this bloody war to be over.

It's so hot here, Lily. Sometimes we don't think we can bear another day. Our uniforms are so thick and scratchy, there are flies everywhere, and the bit of food we manage to get always makes us ill. Most of the boys have had dysentery. Do you remember old Johnny Smith from Spitalfields Market? He dropped dead the other day, right in front of our eyes. Oh Lily, you wouldn't believe what I've seen out here. Human beings at their very worst and their very best. It certainly makes me realise what a good life we had back at home. The poverty here is dreadful, just as bad if not worse than in the roughest slums in London. But the local people have been quite nice to us. We've been charged with protecting the Suez Canal, and some of the boys have started constructing roads and a railway. There's talk that we'll be pushing into Palestine after that. I don't know if that's true, but it makes me very uneasy. I just want to come home to you and my baby son.

Hope you are doing okay living with Mum and Rose. I do worry about you girls being all alone now that me and the boys are gone. Have you had any word from Albert or John? We got split up after training. I thought they were on the same ship as me, but then heard they were on the next one. Talk is that they were being sent straight into the desert.

Oh Lily, it's nothing like they promised us. There's no glory, just heat, sickness, and melancholy. Some of the lads are even talking about doing away with themselves; they just can't see an end to it all. We thought we'd be home by Christmas, but the way things are going it looks like we'll be in this hell hole a lot longer than that. Mind you, we lads are sticking together. All us Cockneys get together sometimes and sing the old songs from home; **It's A Long Way To Tipperary, Pack Up Your Troubles In Your Old Kit Bag, and Keep the Home Fires Burning** *are our favourites. You should hear the lads belting those out. If we close our eyes while we're singing we can almost imagine we're home, back in Old Blighty, in those old lanes and alleys we know so well. I tell you Lily, we may be fighting for King and Country, but I wish I'd never signed up. I hate this country, I hate the army, I hate it all. I just want to be safely home with you and baby Henry.*

Sorry this letter has been a bit of a long moan... I will write again as soon as I can scrounge some paper and a decent pen, both those things are a bit short out here.

Sending you all my love.
Valentine

Lily never received this long, heartfelt letter. It was deemed by the army censors to be too informative, too precise, and far too melancholy. It was critical that the folks back home–the entire population of England–thought the war was going well. It was vital to public morale that the message be sent of soldiers doing well–even having an adventure on the battlefield.

London 1916

My Darling Valentine,

I do hope this letter finds you well. I can't believe we have been apart so long, I do hope this war ends soon.

I have some very sad news. Our darling baby Henry died last week without you even meeting him. He was thriving, toddling around and smiling, then he suddenly got sick and died before we could even get him to the hospital. I am so sorry, Valentine. I tried so hard to protect our boy until you came home to us.

Your loving wife,
Lily

London 1917

My dear brother Valentine,

I do hope this finds you well. We are so worried about you, as we have heard nothing since that little brown card you sent Lily at Christmas. Apart from saying it was posted in Egypt, we know now about what you're up to. The three of us are very scared. We just want you to come home safe to us.

We were all very upset when little Henry died. He was such a grand little lad, your boy, kept us all in fits of laughter with his antics. He was beginning to do so well. He talked like a real little Cockney, copying all the old men down at the market. We really miss seeing all the young men around; London just seems to be full of women, children, and old men now. All you fit young men are off to war.

Your Lily is struggling a bit. She cries all the time and has done so ever since we put your poor baby into the ground. We managed to get him a nice little plot at Finchley Cemetery, so at least you'll have somewhere to visit him when you get home.

No news of our John or Albert, so you can imagine how Mum worries. Every day we hear of another lad killed out there, someone's son or brother.

I'm still working at Lyons Corner House, although of course, it's all a bit different than what it used to be with it being the war and everything. The company has even opened a hotel, the Regent Palace. It's huge and very grand. When the war's over, I might even try to get a job there.

Mum is all right, although she seems to be getting smaller every day. It's almost like she's shrinking with all the worry.

Anyway, that's all the news for now. We are praying for you and the boys to come home safely to us soon.

Your loving sister,
Rose

London 1917

My dear son Valentine,

It is with a very heavy heart that I write this letter.

We just heard today that your brother John was killed in action at a place called Gallipoli. Apparently it took them a long time to notify us, as there were so many casualties there. It seems that he and all the other brave lads who died have already been buried in that foreign soil.

Oh son, my heart is breaking. I have already lost two boys in babyhood; now John has gone too. I am so worried about you and Albert. I have heard nothing from him, apart from a letter he sent me when he first got out there. I haven't heard much from you either and it just breaks my heart to think of you both out there, fighting in a foreign land, with no-one who loves you close by.

Your Lily is improving a bit. She has got some of her strength back after losing the little one. I was very worried about her for a long time. She was so very unhappy. But Olga and I have been getting her to help us with our sewing, and that seems to have really perked her up. She is getting quite good at it. The other day she covered 42 buttons in silk; now they are ready to be sewn onto a wedding gown Olga is making. It seems to be taking her mind off everything for a bit, thank God.

Your sister Rose keeps us amused. Every day she comes home from work with another story about the people she serves there. So many funny stories, she has us in stitches sometimes! She seems to have taken a fancy to a young man called Cyril. She brought him home to tea the other day and he seems very nice. We were lucky that she managed to bring home some fancy cakes from the restaurant, otherwise we wouldn't have had anything to feed the poor chap!

Anyway Valentine, I must close now. These dresses won't sew themselves, even with your Lily's help.

Try to keep your chin up, son. One day you will be back here with us all, and that day can't come soon enough for me.

Your loving mother,
Martha

London 1918

Hello Son, my little Valentine George,

Thank you for the lovely postcard from Palestine. It arrived this morning, although I daresay you posted it ages ago. I liked the pictures on the front, the ship, the water, the joined hands and the words: **"Greetings from the Holy Land. Far across the deep blue ocean, turn my thoughts to home and you. Longing for your words of greeting and your heart so staunch and true. Day by day I wish to see you, but although** *this cannot be, still of you I'm ever thinking, as I know you think of me."*

Oh son, those words made me cry. I miss you so much, my beautiful boy. I have propped the card up on the mantelpiece above the range, that way I can look at it all the time.

I do hope this finds you well. Rose, your Lily, and I are all doing ok, but of course we long for news of you and your homecoming. They say the war will be over soon. I hope so. So many lives lost... and for what? All those fit young men taken in their prime.

I have some more sad news. We heard yesterday that your brother Albert has been found alive, in a hospital in France. They say he is very sick, shell shocked or something, and he is being sent home as soon as they can get him on a ship. I can't wait to see my boy, but I don't know what I'll find when I do. So many lads from 'round here are coming back with missing limbs or their minds destroyed. I just hope our Albert is one of the lucky ones. Will let you know as soon as we hear anything.

Oh son, apart from that lovely postcard on which you just wrote, **To Mother, from Valentine George,** I don't suppose the censors would let you say any more. It has been a whole year now since we heard anything from you. Your Lily always looks so sad when we mention your name. It seems so unfair that you were married for such a short time before they carted you off to war. I know it was your choice to enlist, but I think the government was wrong to pretend it was all going to be such a great adventure. If you boys had known what you were really going to face, I bet none of you would have signed up. It makes my blood boil, a whole generation of young men thrown on the rubbish tip.

Anyway son, I'd better close now. There might be one bit of good news. Our Rose seems to be getting very friendly with that Cyril, so there might be wedding bells soon. I really hope so; he is a lovely lad.

Take care of yourself. Hopefully we will all be together again soon.

Your loving mother,
Martha

London December 1918

My darling Valentine,

Every day since Armistice Day I have prayed for your speedy return. So many of the other lads have come home already, although quite a lot, like Albert, are very badly damaged.

He was in a convalescence place down in Worthing for a couple of months before we got him home the other week. He looks the same—apart from his missing arm—but his mind has gone a bit. He can still talk normally, but he has fits sometimes, and every night he has nightmares about what happened out there. Apparently, out of his platoon there were only three who survived. He must have seen some dreadful things, Valentine, to keep upsetting him like this. We are just hoping that being back here with us, the family who love him, will help him to mend.

I am enjoying helping your mum and Olga with their sewing. They have started giving me more intricate work to handle and I love it. Do you remember that when we first met, I told you I always wanted to be a seamstress? Well now I am! I hope you will be proud of me when you see my work.

There has been so much loss here. So many of our neighbours have lost their sons and brothers. My own brother Tom was killed at Gallipoli like your John, but it seems Dick and Harry have been saved and will be home soon.

I so long for news of you, my darling husband. Every night I pray that you will return safely to me and that we will be able to start making our own little family. I miss our baby Henry every day and visit his grave whenever I can.

Godspeed to you my darling. Come home safely to me now this dreadful war is over.

Your loving wife,
Lily

Valentine never received these letters, well, not in their entirety. The censors had used their thick black pens to hide most of the words, leaving only the bare essentials and deleting anything that might get into enemy hands and affect the course of war.

Thus, he only knew that his baby son had died, one of his brothers was killed at Gallipoli, and the other had returned home a broken man.

Valentine went home to London in 1919, and he was completely changed. A man changed by his experiences, as were so many others who had survived the terrible war.

CAMDEN TOWN
LONDON 1921

Valentine George looked down at the crisp one pound note in his hand and smiled. One pound.

Twenty whole shillings he had never expected to earn today. One of the families he had done a house removal for had been so pleased with his work that they had tipped him generously. Both Valentine and the old driver, Sam, had been given one pound each. And he knew exactly what he was going to do with his share.

First, he was going to buy four loaves of nice fresh bread– one for Lily, one for his mum, one for Olga, and one for his mother-in-law, Sarah. He would pop in and deliver them as soon as he got home. He might also take them some fresh fish if he got to the market in time; his mum was partial to a nice bit of haddock. And some jellied eels for their Albert, he would enjoy those. If there was anything left, he would buy a bunch of violets for Lily.

Everything had changed after he got home from the war.

It had taken him quite a while to readjust to life in civvy street. He had become so used to the discipline of being a soldier. He was now shocked by some of the things he saw around him. So many of his old school friends never made it back home. They were lost, buried in some distant, foreign land, leaving their mothers grieving forever. He saw how the loss of John had affected his mum. Although she always tried to put a brave face on her troubles, he couldn't help but notice how often she looked at the framed photo of his dead brother, tears rolling down her face. At least Albert had come home. Not quite whole exactly, due to his missing arm and shell-shocked mind, but he was here. They could all hug him and hold him when he had nightmares. None of them could sleep through those; his screams echoed around the house, waking them all from their slumber. Valentine could only imagine the horrors his brother had seen. He had experienced enough himself, watching his mates lose their minds as rats ran across them at night in the trenches, or looking on in horror as fellow soldiers were killed by enemy gunfire right in front of him. He knew that most men who had been through those things would never be the same again, would never return to being the carefree young men they had been before the war.

He was so lucky. He had his Lily and their new baby. Little Lily Rose was nine weeks old now and the apple of his eye. He was quite convinced that she was the most beautiful baby there had ever been. Having her had taken away a bit of their sorrow at losing Henry back in 1916. Of course they would never "get over it"; losing a child was the worst thing that could possibly happen to anyone. But at least now, he could go to the cemetery and sit by little Henry's grave without wailing so loudly that passers-by would stop and stare. Just last week, they had taken baby Lily to Finchley Cemetery with them and they had talked to her quietly, telling her all about her big brother, the brother who was now in Heaven, the brother whom she would never meet on Earth.

Valentine had been back from war for nearly a year before he and Lily began talking about making a second baby. Both of them were scared, scared to love another little person that might be taken away from them, but in the end they decided they must be brave.

Lily Rose was born at home, surrounded by her loving family. The family had changed a bit in the last year. They were no longer living in the tenement block in the slums, but now spent their days in a four-storey house on Georgiana Street in Camden Town. As his mum always said, "Life changes when you least expect it to."

She was right. None of them could have ever imagined their lives changing like this.

They had the whole house to themselves! A nice house in a nice neighbourhood. Not far from Regent's Park. Not far from Camden High Street. Light-years away from the slums. It was still a working-class area of course, full of hardworking folks just trying to support their families, but it wasn't the slums. The air was cleaner, the streets were well lit, there were no public houses in sight; you had to walk a couple of blocks if you fancied a pint.

Valentine often had to pinch himself when thinking about how it happened. A couple of months after his return from Palestine, Rose came home from work visibly excited. She had always been a rather theatrical girl so they were well used to her dramatic entrances, but this was different.

"You lot won't believe what happened today." She paused, waiting for them all to pay attention.

"One of my regulars came in at lunchtime yesterday with a friend of his, some colonel or something. I was just serving them like I always do. They ordered ham, egg, and chips, and I heard the old man talking about being in Palestine. I told him about you two being soldiers and about our John getting killed at Gallipoli. They were really nice, let me waffle on a bit, 'til Ada, our stuck-up supervisor, came over to find out why I was taking so long. Anyway, they came back today, both of them, and asked me if I could meet them for a drink when my shift finished. I told them I couldn't 'cos I was meeting Cyril, my fiancée, so they said to bring him along too."

She paused again, ensuring she had their full attention before she continued.

"Anyway, I told them how Cyril and I were getting married soon and that I was worried you wouldn't be able to manage without my money now that John is gone and our Albert isn't really well enough to get a proper job."

They all waited.

"It turns out that the colonel went to school with Cyril's brother, so they already knew each other, and he was really sad hearing about all our bad luck–Dad dying, our two little brothers gone before their second birthdays, Robert running away to seek his fortune in Africa, losing our John in the war, and all Albert's horrible injuries. I even told them about you and Lily losing your baby while you were in Egypt, Valentine. By the time I'd finished there was hardly a dry eye in the house."

"Oh Rose love, do you really have to air all our family secrets in public?"

"Mum, they're not secrets, everyone knows about them. Anyway, just wait 'til you hear the next bit."

"Okay love, what's the next bit?"

If Rose could have found a stage right at that moment, she would have leapt on it and turned on all the spotlights.

"He's offered us a house... if we want it. To rent for less than it's worth. He just wants to help a family whose young men sacrificed so much for their country."

Apparently this man, who shall remain nameless as he requested, felt incredibly guilty that he had survived the war while so many young men under his command had perished. He was independently wealthy, having inherited land and property from various rich relatives, and he felt strongly that it was now time to give something back. He had been looking for a family to help, and it just so happened that he had met Rose at exactly the right time. The fact that he also knew Cyril helped too.

And so it was done. They all moved to Georgiana Street, Camden Town. The house, built in about 1850, was a four-storey terraced house built of yellow stock brick, with white stucco on the lower half. Decorative black wrought-iron railings led up to the front door and down a few steps to the basement, and the first floor windows had little matching balconettes. It was the end house in the long terrace and was next to an archway that led to a cobbled mews. Beyond the mews was an old factory. It was a stark contrast to the dark and dingy little rooms in the slums.

Martha couldn't bear to leave behind her good friends, so Olga and Svetlana moved into the ground floor rooms. Martha, Rose, and Albert took over the first floor, while Valentine, Lily, and baby Lily Rose had the top floor. That left the basement empty.

Lily's mum and two remaining brothers were struggling to survive in Stanhope Street. With one less wage coming in now their Tommy was dead, it was really hard for them to manage to find the rent every week. They often had to hide in the kitchen when the landlord came round, wincing when he tapped loudly on the window before yelling that he would give them one more week to pay the arrears or they were out on their backsides.

Sarah had sobered up during the war. With the boys away fighting there were no wages coming in and certainly nothing to buy gin or snuff with. She had found a few small cleaning jobs just to keep body and soul together, and although her sister Mabel refused to give her any more cash knowing she would probably waste it on drink, she did appear every week with a basket full of fresh produce from her little garden. Lily helped her mum too; even though she had gone to live with Valentine's family, she was a good daughter and went home religiously each Sunday to visit.

After they had all moved into the new house and were comfortably settled, they felt a little guilty at living in such relative luxury while others were struggling. The basement, which was approached by stairs leading straight from the street, consisted of one big kitchen and two smaller rooms at the back. It was a little dark and gloomy, but it was clean and dry and they could rent it out very cheaply thanks to the generosity of their benefactor. Dick and Harry had both worked for a house removal company before the war and their old boss welcomed them back with open arms upon their return. He kept his horses in the mews stables behind Georgiana Street, so when he heard that their brother-in-law, Valentine, had moved into the street, was looking for a job, and was good with horses, he offered him a position. It was the perfect fit. Valentine would be living right next door to the stables, so could keep an eye on the horses, making sure they were fit for work every day and helping out with removals when necessary. It wasn't an especially well-paid position, but he thought it was just wonderful.

"Your brothers have been so good recommending me for this job, Lily. It would have taken me ages to find anything half as good. But I do feel bad that they are still living in that dump in Stanhope Street while we are all living it up here."

And so, after much discussion, it was decided that they would offer the basement rooms to Sarah, Dick, and Harry.

They were, of course, delighted to accept the invitation. It was a chance for a new start in a much better environment, and with family at hand. Soon, Lily's mum and brothers moved their few meagre possessions to Georgiana Street and together, they all began a new life.

Three weeks after Valentine enjoyed spending the unexpected pound tip for the house removal job, his baby Lily Rose got sick.

At first it was just a bit of a temperature, which the family put down to teething. The next day, she had a raging fever and wouldn't eat. She was sleepy all the time, and when she was awake she cried constantly, obviously in pain.

By the second day, Valentine could bear it no more and sent for the doctor. They couldn't really afford it, but little Lily Rose was doing too poorly to be brought all the way to the hospital. The doctor came, demanded his sixpence fee before he would even look at the child, and then pronounced that she was obviously unwell. He said it was probably diphtheria, that there was nothing he could do, and that she would almost certainly be dead by the morning.

And that was exactly what happened. Little Lily Rose died in the arms of her loving, distraught family at the age of just 12 weeks. Valentine and Lily had lost their second child to a cruel disease, knowing that if they had had enough money to afford a better doctor, their precious little girl might have been saved.

In the dark days that followed little Lily Rose's death, the rest of the family had been worried that her parents would lose their minds. To have lost two much-wanted children in such awful ways was such a terrible burden to bear.

At the funeral they had both wept loudly, not caring what anyone thought. They both wanted to jump in the grave with the tiny white coffin that held their precious baby. They had managed to get a plot right next to little Henry, and every day for the first six months after Lily Rose passed, her mother went to the cemetery to be with her babies. She had dark circles under her eyes from all the crying and was completely listless. She dragged herself out of bed every day and spent all of the daylight sitting by her children's graves, talking to them, singing lullabies, half-losing her reason. Someone always went with her; none of them could bear the idea of her grieving alone. Valentine couldn't always go of course, he had to muster the energy to get himself to work every day and earn money to support them. Sometimes the horses would be wet with his tears as the grief overtook him.

Lily couldn't even be persuaded to do any sewing. Martha and Olga had set up a little sewing room on the ground floor. Olga and Svetlana didn't need all the space they had in the apartment, so it seemed sensible to use some as a workroom. By the time they had finished giving it a lick of paint and some pretty curtains at the window, the little room became not just a workspace, but also a showroom of sorts, a place for their customers to come and be measured or have fittings. Dick and Harry brought home some old timber they had picked up at the scrapyard and Valentine and Albert had used it to build a big table and some shelving. The women were thrilled with their new space; it was such a contrast to their old place in the slums where they had been forced to work in a chilly, gloomy, and damp room lit only by candlelight. Here in Georgiana Street, the light flooded in through the big windows, making it easy to see what they were stitching.

"Oh Olga, I'm so worried about that girl. She just doesn't seem to be getting any better. I don't think going down to the cemetery every day is really helping her. I just don't know what to say anymore. Nothing seems to do any good. We're all at our wits' end. And she's getting so thin, just wasting away. Valentine says she barely eats anything at all."

"Martha, of course you are worried. We all are."

Olga, the old Russian lady and Martha's friend of so many years, spoke gently.

"But I think we must take special care of her now."

"What do you mean Olga? We're all doing nothing but taking care of her."

"It isn't really my place to say Martha, but I think she might be expecting again. There's just something about the way she sits, and have you noticed she keeps refusing to drink any tea or coffee? Even that fancy old Camp Coffee in a bottle that your Valentine likes so much. She used to quite like that stuff.

I can't stand it of course, not my cup of tea at all. I expect Valentine just got used to drinking that foreign muck when he was in the army."

"Oh Olga, you are funny. Foreign muck indeed! Do you really think Lily's in the family way?"

"I do, Martha. Mark my words, I'm sure I'm right."

And she was. Just a few weeks later, Lily and Valentine announced her pregnancy to the family.

"I expect you all think it's too soon after losing our little Lily Rose."

"We never intended it. It seems a bit disrespectful to her memory somehow, having another baby so soon. Like we're trying to replace her."

Lily sounded very tearful.

"I didn't realise I was expecting 'til the other day. I'd lost so much weight and nothing was working properly, but then I realised when the baby started kicking me. I think it's due in about three months."

Martha was anxious. Lily was not really in a fit state, neither physically nor emotionally, to have another baby. She was still grieving. But it was too late to change anything now; they all just had to be as supportive as they possibly could be. At least they had a decent home for this baby. This one wouldn't be born in the slums, perhaps that meant it would be stronger, better able to fight off sickness and disease.

Martha became increasingly anxious about Lily giving birth. Childbirth was such a risky business. Two of her own sisters had died that way. Admittedly, neither of them had been in great health, having spent all their working lives at the Bryant and May match factory. They had been forced to work long hours there, sometimes up to 14 hours a day, inhaling dreadful fumes. A few of the girls they worked with had developed the dreaded phossy jaw, which was often fatal for those who could not afford treatment.

Martha had only been 15 years old when both her sisters died within weeks of each other. They had both been so excited about becoming mothers and often talked about how their children "won't be going to no match factory; they'll get an education and get proper jobs."

They had both gone into labour in the slums, in the rooms where Martha had grown up.

Betty, the eldest at 19, had died trying to give birth to a baby fathered by her 20-year-old husband. She had been so frightened and had cried out in terror every time she had a painful contraction. The midwife, who reeked of gin, had refused to send for a doctor until it was too late, even though she knew there was a problem. Martha, her mother, and her sister Liza, had all stood by the bed, watching helplessly as Betty tried pushing with all her might. She fought right to the end, but her little boy was born dead and she followed him just half an hour later.

Liza was only 17. She had married her childhood sweetheart a week earlier, desperate for her child to be born "in wedlock." After watching her older sister die so horribly, she was naturally terrified when she went into labour in the very same room and the very same bed, although this time, a different midwife was in attendance. It all started out well. She was coping with the pain and they all expected it to be over quickly, a healthy baby tucked safely in her arms. But there were complications. The baby, a healthy little boy, was safely born, introduced to his proud father. Then everything went horribly wrong. His mother, that apparently healthy 17-year-old woman, bled to death.

Martha had never forgotten that awful time. Every time she gave birth to one of her own babies she had remembered her sisters and their suffering. It made her so very emotional, angry- and full of despair driven by seeing her sisters and countless other women die needlessly just because they were too poor to afford a doctor.

So she worried about Lily, Valentine, and the prospect of this new baby. She knew how much her boy loved his wife, and how devastated he would be if anything happened to her. She also knew just how emotionally fragile they both were, having already lost two precious children.

Luckily all her fears were unfulfilled. Baby Doris Elizabeth was born a few weeks later, just 10 months after her Lily Rose had died.

Exactly eleven months after that, a baby son, John George was born. A healthy, happy little boy who finally made Valentine and Lily's family complete.

FINCHLEY CEMETERY
LONDON 1925

Valentine George clutched the hands of his two small children.

Doris Elizabeth was now three years old; her little brother John was two. They both stood with their father by the open graveside looking pale and frightened, watching as their mother's coffin was lowered into the dark hole. All around them people wept, unable to control their emotions at the utter unfairness of it all.

Just two years ago, Lily Rose Scarborough finally got the happiness she so desperately wanted and deserved: a loving husband returned safely from the horrors of war and two beautiful children who had survived infancy. Her life had seemed charmed. She and Valentine were so happy together, her children were thriving, and everyone living in the house in Georgiana Street was content, going about their business and making the best of what they had been given. Unfortunately, everyone's joy only lasted a short time.

Lily had started to feel tired six months earlier. Not just the normal kind of "tired" that one would get running a home and looking after two active children, but a bone-weary kind of tired. She began losing quite a bit of weight along with her appetite–even though Valentine tried to tempt her with her favourite things. The pain in her back just wouldn't go away, and although she was secretly worried, she tried to carry on as usual. She did not want to make a fuss. One day she collapsed in the street on her way home from the market, all the shopping from her basket lying on the pavement. One of their neighbours who had been peering as usual through her lace curtains, rushed out to help her.

"I really think she should go to the hospital, Martha. She just collapsed, dropped down in a heap right in front of my very eyes! Lord knows what would have happened to her if I hadn't noticed."

The next day Valentine insisted on taking his Lily to the hospital. Like most poor people, they only went to hospital as a last resort, only if they were really sick or had broken a bone. They both hated the imposing old brick buildings of St. Pancras Hospital. Part of the building had originally been the old workhouse, and, like most people of their class, they and their ancestors had lived in terror of "going on the parish"– becoming a workhouse inmate.

By the time they got back to Georgiana Street that evening, they were both in despair. The news they had been given was sad and shocking. Lily had chronic kidney disease and the doctors could do nothing for her. They predicted that at her young age of 30 years old, she might have another year, at most, to live.

Sadly, the doctor's prognosis was miscalculated. The precious young woman, a much-loved wife and mother to two small children, died just four months later, two weeks before her 31st birthday. She was buried in a grave at Finchley Cemetery, finally getting to be alongside her two dead babies.

Valentine felt as though his heart was completely broken, shattered into a million pieces by the sudden loss of his wife. He had loved her for so long, and yet they had managed to have so little precious time together between the war and losing their babies. For the first six months after Lily died he struggled to get up every day, struggled to take care of Doris Elizabeth and John. His only solace was going out to attend to the horses. Alone with them in the darkness of the stables he could cry, releasing bits and pieces of his anger and pain from the last few months. He tried not to cry in front of his children; they were traumatised enough. Months after Lily's funeral they were still asking when their mum was coming home.

Martha and Albert took care of the children every day while Valentine worked. He knew they were in good hands with his family, safe and well loved. Every night as he tucked them into bed, little Doris would say her prayers:

"Dear Jesus, please send my mum home soon. We miss her." Each time the words left her mouth, his heart would break even more. Then, she would sing the hymn she had learnt at the ragged school in her tiny, sweet voice, *All Things Bright and Beautiful.* It had been Lily's favourite, one she learnt as a child and had sung to her children almost every day when they were babies.

Valentine tried to remember all the good memories–the sunny summer days when they had all strolled to Regent's Park, the children's excitement at visiting the zoo, sitting on the grass listening to the music being played in the bandstand. How Lily had loved all those band concerts; she had nagged him every summer weekend to go and listen. He remembered Saturday mornings spent at Camden Market or visiting Lily's Aunty Mabel at her house by Regent's Canal. He smiled sadly as he pictured watching her laughing as she sat downstairs with his mum and Olga, sewing beautiful dresses. At least she had been able to realise that dream of hers, to be a seamstress.

He thought of the quiet evenings he had spent with his beloved girl, sitting in front of a roaring fire, chatting quietly about their hopes and dreams for the future. Talking about their ambitions for their two precious children who were tucked into bed, fast asleep in the next room. It had never occurred to either of them that they wouldn't grow old together. He remembered Lily on their wedding day; she had been so shy and beautiful and he had felt like the luckiest man alive. She had been a wonderful mother, devoting every spare moment she had to little Doris and John. And now, she was gone. All they had left were memories.

CAMDEN TOWN
LONDON 1929

"Uncle Albert, will you please show me how to draw an elephant?"

Albert grinned at the little girl sitting at the kitchen table beside him.

"Of course I will, my love, although I'm not really sure if I know how to draw elephants."

"Grandma says that my Uncle Robert lives in Africa, where all the wild animals are. I bet he knows how to draw them."

"I'm quite sure he does, Dot, maybe one day he'll come back to England! Then he can tell us all about them himself."

Doris Elizabeth, beloved daughter of Valentine and the late Lily, had grown into a bright, intelligent little girl. She had just celebrated her seventh birthday and was so loved by everyone around her.

She announced when she was just five years old that she hated the name "Doris," and wished she had been called Elizabeth instead. As a compromise, she had agreed to the nickname "Dot," and that is how she had been known ever since.

"I hope I can go to Africa one day. Or India or China, or Egypt or Palestine. My dad was in Egypt and Palestine during the war, you know. And you were at a place called Gallipoli, weren't you Uncle Albert? Is that where you hurt your arm?"

Albert smiled to himself. What a sweet girl she was, so naive and loving and kind. Referring to the arm he had lost in the war as just "hurt."

"When I grow up, I'm going to see the world. I want to be an artist like you. Maybe we could go together? I promise I will be really good and do everything you tell me. We would have such fun!"

"Now, now Dot, don't pester your uncle. He's got an important job to finish. Mrs.Fiskett wants that picture of her grandson done by Sunday, in time for his christening."

Albert smiled at his mum. Martha was so sweet, always fussing over him, always trying to find him work, little commissions to keep him occupied so he didn't have too much time to think about how different his life might have been if he hadn't gone to war and lost his arm. At least the nightmares had faded a bit now. He didn't wake up screaming every single night, reliving the horrors he had seen in the trenches and on the battlefield. It had been ten years since he was sent home a wrecked and broken man, but thanks to the love and support of his family, he had survived. He continued to improve year by year. Honestly, he had to give a lot of the credit for that to the little girl beside him at the table. Since the minute she could walk she had been his constant companion, always by his side, always asking questions and telling him of her plans for the future. And what big plans she had for such a little one!

Dot was also very close to her Aunty Rose. Although Rose had moved away when she married Cyril, she was a constant visitor to the house, especially since Lily had died. In many ways, she had become like a second mother to the little girl, and so some of her strongly-held views were now quoted often.

"Aunty Rose says that women are definitely equal to men, and that it is nonsense they have to give up their jobs when they get married. She says that men don't have to, so why should they?"

"Aunty Rose says that girls should have the same education as boys. She says that lots of girls are smarter than boys anyway, they just don't get the chance to show it 'cos they have to be wives and mothers instead."

The little girl quoted her aunt verbatim and it made the others laugh. Half the time she probably didn't even understand exactly what she was saying, but she said it anyway.

"Aunty Rose says that when I grow up, I can be whatever I want to be–do any job I like–and so I'm going to be a famous artist like Uncle Albert. Then we are going to travel the world and make a fortune selling our paintings."

"My teacher says I am quite good at drawing and writing, so I think I can easily do it."

"Look Grandma, I've just done this picture of my mum, what do you think? Does it look like her?"

Dot had copied the photo they kept of her mum on the mantelpiece. In it, Lily was staring straight at the camera, a slight smile on her pretty face. She was wearing a high-necked lace blouse and on her head was a large brimmed hat, trimmed with matching lace.

"Oh love, it *is* good. You've really caught your mum's likeness. Your dad will be thrilled when you show it to him once he gets home."

"She was very beautiful, wasn't she Grandma? I do wish I could remember her properly. I always talk to her when I say my prayers at bedtime, but I can't remember what her voice sounded like. I wish I could, I wish she hadn't died. I wish I had a mum like all the other kids at school."

Martha's heart went out to the little girl. She was such a sweet child, so brave, kind, and loving. It was tragic that she had lost her mum at such a young age.

"Our John doesn't remember her at all. I s'pose he was too young. I remember standing by her grave in my black coat and wondering why everyone was throwing flowers into the hole. And I remember when she used to take me with her to the market sometimes and we stopped to get an ice-cream."

"Oh, love. She hasn't really left you, she's up there in Heaven looking down on you all the time, making sure you're okay."

The years passed, as they always do, and Lily became a precious memory, someone the family used to know and love, someone who had been in their lives every day but was now missing.

Martha and Olga missed her terribly–her infectious laugh, her enthusiasm for her work as a seamstress, and her gentle, loving manner. She had, under their instruction, become a very proficient dressmaker. Being younger than the others she had been more aware of current fashions, so she ensured that their designs were always in demand. The three of them always had such fun working together, the little workroom was constantly full of happiness.

Down in the basement, Lily's side of the family grieved too. Sarah had lost her only daughter, Dick and Harry lost their beloved sister. Both of Lily's brothers were married now, and their wives had moved in, sharing the rooms with them and their mum. After Lily passed, everyone had expected her to resort to the drink once again, but she had surprised them by turning to religion instead. Every Sunday, she went to the local mission church and seemed to find it of great comfort. She also took care of Dot and John if Martha or Albert were too busy. While everyone's lives continued to change as their memories of Lily became more and more distant, they kept trying to move forward, learning how to be there for Valentine and the children.

LONDON 1930

Time carried on, and life kept transforming for the entire family.

Svetlana had a very severe seizure. For once, no one had been in the room with her when it happened. She had been doing so well as of late that everyone in the house had felt a little more relaxed at the thought of leaving her unattended. By the time Olga came back from her shopping trip, it was too late. Losing Svetlana was a great sadness to them all, another deeply-loved member of their little family gone before her time. Olga was ridden with guilt. She had always taken such good care of her little sister, ever since they had arrived in London after escaping Russia. She was so distraught that Martha insisted she move upstairs into the rooms where she and Albert lived. There was plenty of space there and it meant they could then expand their sewing workshop and showroom. Making clothes proved to be a great solace to them both as they worked through their grief.

A few months later, Valentine came down with rheumatic fever and they thought they were going to lose him too. It happened quite suddenly. He was carted off to the hospital, where he spent weeks hovering between life and death. It was almost as though he had given up, as if the pain of carrying on without his beloved Lily was just too much.

In the end, he rallied, and was sent down to a convalescence home in Bognor Regis. It was thought that the bracing sea air would speed up his recovery. He spent several weeks down there and returned to London looking fitter and healthier than he had in years. He even looked as if he put on a little weight. Martha was delighted to see her son looking so well.

"Mum, I've got something to tell you."

"Oh yes love, what is it? By the way, I thought I'd do some nice sausage and mash for our tea. The kids love it and I know it always used to be your favourite. I got some really nice sausages from that butcher on the high street. We're just happy to have you back son, we missed you so much! Little Dot hardly slept last night, she was so excited at the thought of seeing you."

"Actually Mum, I've met someone."

There was a stunned silence in the kitchen. Only Martha was in the room. The children were in the basement, playing with the wooden train set their Uncle Harry had made for them. Olga and Albert were downstairs, drawing up some new dress designs.

"What kind of someone, Valentine?"

"A lady. Her name is Elizabeth. Elizabeth Silver. She's a widow, lost her husband three years ago."

"Oh, I see." It had never occurred to Martha that her son might meet someone else. He had been so devastated when Lily died. Somehow she had always thought he was a one-woman-man, the kind of man that would only love once in his life. But looking at him now, she realised she was obviously wrong. There was a twinkle in his bright blue eyes that she hadn't seen for many years.

"Did you meet her in Bognor?"

"Yes I did, Mum. She was convalescing too, so we kind of just got chatting every day when we were sitting outside getting fresh air. I'm planning to go and visit her on Sunday, now we're both back in London."

"Where does she live?"

"In Battersea. She lives with her mum and dad, her old grandmother, and her two sons."

"Two sons? How old are they?"

"Tommy is 14 and Harry is nearly 12."

Martha's heart sank. It sounded like he knew a lot about this woman and her family already. She just hoped he wasn't going to do anything rash; he still wasn't truly over Lily.

The next morning, Martha went next door and made a phone call. Her neighbour, Mrs. Pratt, had just had a new telephone installed. Rose and Cyril had gotten one recently too. Usually Martha thought it was an unnecessary waste of money; who knew if these newfangled contraptions would even last? Why couldn't people just be content with writing letters? Today though, she was in a hurry. She needed to get hold of her girl quickly.

"Rose love, could you pop 'round and talk to your brother?"

"Oh Mum, what's Albert been up to now? Talking some poor girl into posing naked for him?"

Martha chuckled, despite herself. Her girl was so funny, always making a joke. She explained her predicament to her daughter, who seemed to think she was overreacting.

"Okay, I'll tell Cyril to make his own tea and I'll pop in about six. What are you having tonight? Will there be enough for me too?"

Whenever Rose walked into a room, it suddenly brightened. She had always been an attractive girl, but now that she was a respectable married woman, her beauty somehow seemed luminous. She was absolutely adored and cosseted by her husband. Nothing was too much trouble for him. He was a quiet, rather shy man, and still couldn't believe that this beautiful, spirited young woman had agreed to become his wife. Not to mention, marrying her had cost him dearly. His wealthy family had disowned him, horrified that he had chosen a girl from the East End–a Cockney waitress–to be his wife. They had expected him to choose someone more like them, a girl from a family with wealth and status, not some little upstart from the slums. They had even heard that she supported women's rights; that was the last straw!

To Cyril, it was all worth it if he got to be with his Rose. He had realised, after knowing her for just a few short weeks, that Rose was his equal, despite the fact that she had not grown up the way he had. Fortunately, his elderly maternal grandmother supported his decision. She had been a suffragette when she was younger and thoroughly approved of the outspoken young woman he had chosen to marry. She gave him enough money to buy a little house, and his job in the city ensured that he could provide his bride with a decent lifestyle. To Rose, who had spent most of her life scrimping and saving just to buy a new Sunday dress, it seemed like a life of absolute luxury and she took to it like a duck to water. She adored Cyril, so they both felt they had achieved their dream.

"So, what's all this about then? What have these boys been up to that you felt the need to drag me here, leaving poor old Cyril to make his own tea?"

Martha was so impressed. Fancy having the confidence to ask… rather, *tell* your husband to get his own tea! She would never in a million years have had the courage to do that.

"Does Cyril mind you not going straight home, love?"

"Oh Mum, of course he doesn't. He's a modern man, he understands that women are his equals. Anyway, he said he would probably pop over here afterwards to walk me home."

Rose and Cyril had bought a little semi-detached villa on a quiet street on the edge of Regent's Park. It was Rose's pride and joy and she kept it absolutely spotless. Martha often thought it was so clean that you could easily eat your dinner off the lino floor.

"Our Valentine has met a lady."

"Oh Mum, that's good! Isn't it? You wouldn't want him to be on his own forever; he's been so miserable since Lily died. And those kids could probably do with having a mother figure."

Martha bristled. Good thing Valentine wasn't home from work yet to hear his sister's words! She had always been full of her own opinions, that one.

How dare she speak as though Dot and John didn't have a mother figure? Who did Rose think had been looking after them for the last few years?

Rose noticed the look on her mother's face and realised what she had implied. "Oh Mum, I know you've been doing a wonderful job since Lily died. Dot and John love you, of course, but you're a bit old to be chasing two little ones around. They probably need someone a bit younger looking after them."

Valentine came home, hugged his children, and walked into the rather chilly atmosphere of his mum's kitchen.

"Hello Rose. I didn't know you'd be here tonight. Good to see you. Where's that husband of yours? Fed up with you already?"

Rose poked her brother gently and laughed.

"He'll never be fed up with me, he knows a good thing when he sees it. Anyway, I'm here to talk about you, not me."

"What do you mean? Oh. I get it. Mum's told you about Elizabeth."

"Well, she's only told me the basics, that she's a widow with two kids and that you met her down in Bognor. Is it serious, are you walking out with her?"

Trust Rose to get straight to the heart of the matter. Martha sat at the kitchen table, her head resting on her elbows, watching in admiration as her daughter began her interrogation.

"Well, what did her husband die of? She's not one of those nasty money-grabbing women, I hope? Not that she'd have much luck with you, Valentine, don't suppose you've got two pennies to rub together!

Does she know about your little Dot and John? Are you sure she'd be a good stepmother to them?

Lily would turn in her grave if you brought someone unsuitable into their lives. How well do you really know her? What kind of family does she come from?"

Poor Valentine was flustered, but he understood why his mum and sister were worried. If it was just about him, they probably wouldn't care too much about the people he became involved with. However, he knew they were anxious about his children. Anxious that he would be swept off his feet by some unsuitable floozy who would care nothing about his two motherless children.

"Actually Rose, she's a very nice, respectable woman. She was widowed a few years back and has brought her two boys up on her own. She lives in a house in Battersea with some of her other family members and I'm planning to go and visit her on Sunday. I might even take Dot and John with me."

"Why don't you invite her here first? Maybe ask her and her boys to lunch here on Saturday. Then, we can all meet her. Cyril and I could bring some nice cakes!"

Elizabeth Silver and her sons, Tommy and Harry, accepted the invitation. They were welcomed to Georgiana Street by Martha that very next Saturday afternoon. Everyone crowded into the kitchen on the first floor, where a buffet lunch had been prepared and laid out. The best white linen cloth covered the old pine table, which groaned under the weight of all the food. There were cold meats, salads, bread, and more. Rose had outdone herself with the selection of fancy cakes and Martha had spent the last half hour stopping little John from taking surreptitious bites out of them.

Little Dot was wearing her best Sunday dress, it was a pretty shade of pale pink, and she had a matching bow tied in her hair. John had been forced into his sailor suit, but already it was covered in pink icing from the cake he managed to bite into when no one was looking.

"Everyone, this is Elizabeth. And these are her sons, Tommy and Harry."

The two boys looked very uncomfortable. They would much rather have been with their mates, riding their bikes or playing football down the rec. Instead their mum had dragged them here, across the river, to meet up with some strange new family.

"Pleased to meet you all, I'm sure." She spoke in a quiet voice, rather cultured, with no trace of the East End.

"Glad to make your acquaintance, Elizabeth. Welcome. Sit down and make yourself at home. You too boys; I expect you're starving having come all this way."

Like most East Enders, Martha never ventured south of the River Thames. It seemed like another world to her, somewhere she had no desire to visit. She had worked with a girl once who lived in Southwark, but to Martha that might as well have been France. She hadn't always been this way; when she was young, she had been more adventurous. There had even been a time when she thought she would like to see the world, but those dreams had been knocked out of her long ago. Life had been such a struggle, with little or no time for such frivolous notions. Now, she was content where she lived and worked and saw no reason to change.

"Oh actually Martha, it's not too much of a journey. We just walked over Battersea Bridge, then picked up the bus. Didn't take us too long at all. We enjoyed it, didn't we boys? Seeing all the sights. I don't often get up west these days."

After lunch, Albert took Tommy and Harry into his room to see his model airplanes. He had spent hours making them from balsa wood. Little John trailed behind them of course, desperate to be one of the "big boys."

Dot, however, had no intention of leaving the warmth of the kitchen. She perched herself on a cushion on the floor, right next to her dad's new friend, Elizabeth. She listened carefully to all the talk around her, never once taking her eyes off the woman who bore the same name as her. Suddenly, she returned to loving the name, loving everything about it. She studied the woman's clothing, the pale-green satin dress with a fashionable dropped waist. The matching cloche hat, now removed and sitting on the small table beside her. The pearls around her slim neck. The tiny gold watch.

"Dot, do you like school?"

She suddenly realised that the beautiful creature was addressing her.

"Umm, yes I do."

"And what are your best subjects? Do you have any favourite lessons?"

By the end of the afternoon, the little girl was besotted. No one had ever taken such an interest in her before.

"Dad, are you going to marry that lady?"

"Oh Dot, you shouldn't ask questions like that. Your dad hardly knows her."

Martha spoke sharply, but only because she was worried. She had noticed the affectionate looks that passed between her son and Mrs. Silver, and had realised that their "friendship" was a little more serious than she had thought. Obviously they had become quite close at the convalescent home, with no family to distract them. Still, she supposed, it was early days. She didn't need to worry. After all, it would probably amount to nothing in the end.

BATTERSEA LONDON
1931

Martha had been wrong when she thought it would all come to nothing.

It happened just a few months after that Saturday, the day they had all met Elizabeth and her boys.

Valentine had waited until they were all sitting at the table, eating the Sunday roast she had so lovingly prepared. It was a very special day, because for once she had all her children and grandchildren in one place. Usually someone was missing, they were working overtime, or out visiting their sweethearts, but today was Rose's birthday and she and Cyril had just announced that they were expecting a baby. They had been trying for a whole year with no success, so this was absolutely wonderful news. Martha managed to scrape together enough money to buy a decent-sized chicken and roasted it with a huge pile of potatoes for their lunch. It was a real treat; usually they could only afford a chicken for Christmas or Easter.

"Actually Mum, I have some news too."

Everyone stopped talking and looked expectantly at Valentine.

"I've asked Elizabeth to marry me." He waited for some response, but there was just silence.

"Dot and John will have a new mother figure and two stepbrothers- won't that be grand?"

The room was still silent. Everyone just sat, looking down at the table, avoiding his eyes.

"Isn't anybody going to congratulate me? I thought you'd all be pleased."

"If you get married, does that mean I can call Mrs. Silver 'mum'?"

"Yes it does, Dot. If you'd like." He was so relieved that at least his precious daughter seemed happy at the news, even if the rest of the family didn't.

"If you kids have finished eating, why don't you pop downstairs and see Granny Sarah? I bet she'll let you play with that train set." Martha sounded like she was close to tears.

"We'll call you back up in half an hour or so when the pudding is ready. I've made spotted dick and custard."

Little John leapt out of his seat, delighted to be excused from the boring adult conversation, but Dot was more reluctant to go. This seemed like a very important chat, one she really didn't want to miss even though she knew she wouldn't be allowed any input. As children, even smart girls like her were supposed to be seen and not heard. Normally when her Aunty Rose was visiting, she encouraged Dot to speak out, to say what was on her mind, but today was different. Even *she* could sense that. It sounded like she was going to be getting a new mum, which would be wonderful. Of course, she didn't really know Mrs. Silver very well, but she seemed like a nice lady. It would be great to be the same as all her friends and have a mum of her very own.

She left the room as instructed, but instead of going down to the basement with her brother, she sat quietly on the staircase, listening to every word.

"Oh son, what are you thinking? You haven't known the woman for five minutes. Are you really sure about this?"

"Valentine, I know you miss Lily, but you might be jumping from the frying pan into the fire here. What do you really know about her? About her family?"

"Isn't she a bit old for you?"

"What do her boys think about it? They may not be happy having another man in their lives, seemingly taking the place of their father." "How long has their dad been dead?"

"Does she have her own house? How will you support a big family like that on your wages?"

"Where will you all live? There isn't really room for everyone here, but I daresay we could squeeze them all in if we had to."

Poor Valentine answered his family's questions as best he could. To be honest, he had not expected such a barrage of criticism. Naively, he had expected his family to be happy at the news. He thought they would be happy that he had found someone he could fall in love with again, someone who was excited to be a mother figure to his children.

"Well I'm sorry you all feel this way, but I've made up my mind and she's said yes. We're going to have the banns read next Sunday and we'll get married next month, at her church in Battersea. Of course, I want you all there at the wedding. I thought maybe next Saturday we could all go down there and meet her family. What do you think? They are nice, decent, hardworking people. I think you'll get on with them all right."

The only ones who really enjoyed the wedding were Valentine, little John, and Dot. Even Elizabeth Silver, the bride, was not as relaxed as she might have been; her family, too, had been less than thrilled with the news.

"For goodness sake lass, whatever are you thinking? How do you think those boys of yours are going to take to having a new father figure? They're both still grieving. I know they don't show it, they try to be all tough and manly, but I've heard them both crying in the night. Your Harry still insists on taking his dad's old cap to bed with him every night. Tommy might act like a man now that he's 14, but I reckon he's still a hurt little boy under all that swagger."

"Why do you need another husband anyway? We all rub along all right as we are."

"Will they all come here, or does he expect you to move up north, over the river?"

The way her mother spoke, you would have thought that Camden Town was as far away as Scotland.

"Oh Mum. Don't you want me to be happy? I've been really lonely since Bill died, and Valentine is a good man. I know he'll look after us."

"But what do you really know about him? He hasn't got much of a job, just working in some removal company. He can't earn a very good wage doing that."

"We've managed very well, just us all together in this house. We pay the rent on time and always have enough to put a decent meal on the table every night. Does his family live as well as that, or do you think he's just a gold digger, thinking you are a woman of means?"

"Aunty Alice, don't be so spiteful. Valentine isn't like that. We learnt a lot about each other when we met down in Bognor. Being away from home like that means you have plenty of time to talk. He is a good man and his children are so sweet. Especially his little girl, Dot."

"What kind of name is that, 'Dot'?"

"Her real name is Doris Elizabeth, but everyone calls her 'Dot.' Mind you, she did tell me that now she's met me, she wishes her name was Elizabeth. She is such a dear little thing, so sweet and affectionate. You know I always wanted a daughter."

"Oh Lizzie, wanting a daughter is no reason to marry a man you hardly know. A man much younger than you who doesn't even have his own home and probably can't afford to support you all properly."

Elizabeth's dad, who loved his only daughter passionately, spoke quietly but firmly. He was a soft-spoken man generally, never one to raise his voice or even express his opinion very often. This time though, something compelled him to speak, to say his bit.

"Well my girl, I daresay you're old enough to make up your own mind. But mark my words, this won't end well for either of you. We will help you as much as we can, of course, but I'm not happy. Not happy at all."

Despite the less-than-enthusiastic response from both their families, Valentine and Elizabeth were determined. On a chilly spring afternoon when there was still a trace of snow on the grass, the two were married at the Evangelist Mission Church on Wandsworth Road, followed by a reception at the Old Red House Inn on Stewarts Lane. This was Lizzie's dad's local, the pub he and his mates drank in every Friday night–the same pub he had drunk in every Friday night for the last fifty years. Although he didn't approve of the marriage and he had done this whole thing once before, he was still determined to see his girl off in style. He did a deal with the pub landlord and the party had taken over the whole back room. This way, all the kids could be involved; they certainly wouldn't have been allowed in the main bar. It was a typical London pub party–a few sandwiches and crisps, a wedding cake, and gallons of beer. In the end, even Valentine's family relaxed and enjoyed themselves. He was right, his new in-laws were good, decent, hardworking people, even if they did live on the wrong side of the river!

After the festivities, the bride and groom went off on their honeymoon. They were spending a few days back in Bognor, in a little B&B guesthouse just off the seafront. Little John and Dot said farewell to their new relatives in Battersea and returned home with their family to the house in Georgiana Street.

Battersea
October 1931

Dear Mum,

I hope this letter finds you and the family well. I really miss you all and promise to try and call in next week to see you. It will probably be Thursday; we have a removal job up Hampstead way so I can call in on the way home.

We have all settled in Battersea quite well. Little John is happy, he spends most of his time trailing around after his new brothers. I don't think they like it much, but they are quite kind to him, so I am grateful for that. Dot is thriving. She seems to be blossoming before my eyes. It really suits her, having someone to act as a mother figure again. Lizzie is so good with her, always making sure she is nicely dressed and has good boots and pretty ribbons in her hair. I think she is loving having a little girl around as much as Dot is enjoying being fussed over.

Lizzie's dad seems to have accepted me now. In fact, we have become quite pally and he always insists I join him and his mates at the pub on Friday nights. Her brothers are still a bit quiet around me, but I'm hoping I can win them 'round. Her mum is very nice to me, I think she feels a bit guilty about how she treated me when we first got married. Now that she can see how happy we are, she has relaxed a bit.

Lizzie's Aunty Alice and her husband George, who live on the bottom floor, are so kind. They always make a point of chatting to me and asking how you lot are doing. I think they realise how much I miss you all, how much I miss being in Camden. It's okay here—although the smoke from the power station is a bit much at times, especially if the wind's blowing in the wrong direction. There's a lot of pubs around here, so you see a lot more drunks. Often, little kids are just hanging around outside, waiting for their mums and dads to come home. It breaks my heart.

Anyway, our Dot is now enrolled at the local school, Sleaford Street School, and she seems to love it. She has settled in really well to her new home. She's a bright girl, all the teachers at her new school say so. I am really proud of her. I know how hard it was for you to let my kids go, Mum. You have taken such good care of them since my Lily died, and I really am sorry I had to take them away from you. However, I do think this is for the best. They needed a mother and Lizzie is doing such a lovely job with them.

I really wish you'd all come down to tea one Sunday. I know you hate leaving home, hate crossing the river, but I'd be so happy if you would. Dot and John would love to see you all, I'm sure.

Your loving son,
Valentine

P.S. Give my love and best wishes to all at home. I miss our jolly evenings.

LONDON 1932

Georgiana Street
Camden Town
November 1932

My dear son Valentine,

I was so pleased you managed to pop in and see us last week. You have no idea how much I miss you and those little cherubs. I would go down to visit you in Battersea more often, but I find the bus journey a bit tricky and I don't like leaving our Albert alone too long, in case he has one of his turns. He has been getting a bit worse of late. The nightmares seem to have come back, and I think his missing arm is troubling him. He met a very nice young lady at some place he went to and seemed very keen on her, but once she realised about his arm she lost interest. It seems to have hit him quite hard; I know he would like a wife and kiddies, but somehow I can't see that happening. It's such a shame, 'cos he's a lovely lad with so much to offer the right girl.

I'm sorry to have to tell you that Sarah isn't doing too well. Now that the boys are bringing in a decent wage every week, she has resorted to the old drink again. None of us realised for a while, but then one Friday we heard a lot of yelling from downstairs. It turned out she was up to her old tricks, pawning the boys' best suits again.

Olga is showing her age a bit now. We still do our sewing, but with our arthritis, neither of us are quite as good at it as we used to be. We still get lots of orders, but I think we might soon shut up shop before we are both too decrepit!

Our Rose keeps suggesting that we move in with her and Cyril. They've got plenty of room and I am seriously considering it. Those tenants we got upstairs in your old rooms are okay, but they're a bit noisy and we have to chase them every week for their rent. Albert and Olga are quite keen to move, so I'll let you know what we decide. Rose says that our landlord won't mind, won't be offended if we give him the house back, because then he'll probably sell it and make a pretty profit. We can't complain, he did us such a favour letting us have it cheap all these years. Mind you, I'm also not sure I want to leave. This place has so many memories.

Look after yourself, son. My love to Lizzie, Dot, John, and Lizzie's boys, whom I expect are getting very tall. Isn't Tommy 16 now? And Harry must be what? 13? You are lucky they accepted you, some boys of that age would not stand having another man telling them what to do.

Anyway, I must close now. Have to start making something for tea!

Your loving mother,
Martha

New Road
Battersea
February 1933

Dearest mother,

I do hope this letter finds you all keeping well.

I can't believe you aren't at Georgiana Street anymore. It all happened pretty quickly, didn't it? Trust our Rose to get everything sorted out so fast; that girl is quite something. If she'd been born a boy, she'd probably be running the country by now!

I was glad I could borrow the horse and cart to help you move. Can't believe how much stuff you all had! I think Rose was a bit shocked when all that furniture appeared at her front door. Mind you, she's a good girl; she was very kind to old Olga, making sure she put her favourite chair in exactly the right spot so she could look out the window. And I'm so grateful Mum, for all those bits of furniture you gave Lizzie and me. We really needed a few extra tables and chairs. That lovely Windsor chair Aunty Mabel's husband made will look grand in our new house.

Yes, we're moving! Can you believe it!

This house has been getting a bit crowded, especially now all the kids are getting bigger. Tommy and Harry take up a lot of room with their long legs, They're both nearly six-foot now, they tower over me. Their dad was pretty tall I think, so that's where they get their height from. My little Dot and John are growing like weeds too, although I don't suppose they'll grow much more, as neither me nor their mum have a lot of height. I do miss my Lily. Every time I look at little Dot I am reminded of her. John is more like his mum in terms of looks, but Dot has the same kind and gentle manner that Lily had.

You won't believe how well Dot is doing in school. They say she's very gifted and she's nearly always top of her class in reading, writing, and art. She drew a picture of the old king the other day, in his uniform with all his medals. Mum, she got a really good likeness. Do tell our Albert, he'll be so pleased that she's following in his footsteps.

Anyway, back to the move.

You've probably heard about all this resettlement stuff they're doing to get people out of the slums and into decent housing. Well, I didn't realise that Lizzie had even applied, but apparently she put an application in a few months ago and we just heard yesterday that we've been allocated a council house! It's at a place called Morden, right at the end of the Underground line. It seems they've built hundreds of houses there, just to give families like ours a better life. Honestly, I don't really know how I feel about it, Mum. The city has been home all my life. I found moving here to Battersea hard, I just don't know if I'm brave enough to go all the way out to the country. Lizzie says it will be easy to get back up to town, less than an hour on the Tube, but I'm not so sure. She says I can walk to the station from the new house in about 10 minutes, so it won't take me too long to get to work.

There just seems to be so much change happening right now; I don't like it much. Mostly, I just don't know if it's the right time to move. The boys will be leaving school and getting jobs soon and little Dot is doing so well at the school here. She's due to sit her eleven-plus exam in September and I think she should stay here with Lizzie's mum until she's done it. It could affect her whole future if she passes, give her a real chance to make something of herself. Lizzie says she spoke to the teacher who said it will be all right, that Dot will do well at the new school and can sit the exam there. I guess she has really made up her mind. I can understand that she wants a nice new house with a garden and a bit of space, but I'm not sure she's really thought it through. She's lived all her life here in Battersea. Her family and all her friends are here, and if we move she won't know anybody. I've tried sharing my side, sort of wanting to talk her out of it, but she won't listen much. She says if I really love her, I'll do it. Little John of course is dead keen, he'd follow his step-brothers to the moon if they told him to!

So, it seems Mum, that I'm going to be a country boy again. Maybe it will be like when I was little, when Dad was alive and we stayed down in Hampshire. It was an adventure then, sure, but I had all of you with me—you and Dad, even our Robert. By the way, don't suppose you've heard anything from him since we got that postcard from Johannesburg a couple of years ago? I can't believe he's working in a diamond mine. Shame he got there too late to find his own diamonds, we'd all have been rich now! I wonder if he'll ever come back. If he does, he's sure to bring you a great big sparkler!

Anyway, all being well we are going to be moving in a couple of weeks, so I'll have plenty of time to bring the kids to see you before we go. Maybe next Saturday? Tell Rose to get some nice cakes and I wouldn't mind a bloater sandwich, or some nice jellied eels.

Love to you all. Wish me luck with this new move.

Your loving son,
Valentine

MORDEN, SURREY
OCTOBER 1933

Morden
October 1933

My dear mother,

Well, here we are, stuck at the end of the line, and though I don't love it, I have to say it's not as bad as I thought it might be. It's a bit quiet being surrounded by fields instead of buildings. I miss the clip clop of horse hooves on the cobblestones, and I actually miss all the yelling and screaming when the pubs turn out at night. At the same time I must say, the air is nice and clean here.

I don't like the journey to work much, squashed onto the Tube with all the other workers at six in the morning, but I daresay it could be worse. At least with my new job I don't have to trail across London to get to work anymore, I just hop off the Underground and stroll along to Saville Row. I must say I'm really enjoying the job itself. It was so good of Cyril to recommend me for it. It's much easier work than carting furniture around all day. Gieves is a first-rate company, they make suits for all the upper-class chaps. I think most of the officers from the Royal Navy are kitted out by them. Then there's Hawkes, who supplies the Army chaps. Wouldn't be surprised if one day, they join forces. It would make sense, wouldn't it? Both of them are damn good businesses. Some of the stuff is handmade in their own workshop, but most of it is farmed out to little places in Soho. That's where I often have to go to deliver or pick stuff up. It reminds me of when we were young and you and Olga used to do all that sewing for the aristocracy. Mum, some of these people seem to have a new suit made every five minutes. They're filthy rich, but I must say they're all pretty decent to me. They are especially kind when they hear about what I got up to in the war; they all seem to have respect for us lads who fought in Palestine. I always mention our John too, how he was killed fighting, and how our Albert lost his arm. Somehow, when we all reflect back on and tell our war stories to one another, we become one and the same for a while. Our different classes, whether we've got money or not, none of that seems to matter.

Anyway Mum, I'm glad to hear you are all doing all right. That sister of mine, for all her airs and graces, seems to have turned out pretty well. She's certainly doing a good job looking after you lot and that little Douglas of hers. That little lad is a cheeky one. Last time I dropped in, he hid my hat. Took me ages to find it! It was in the cupboard under the stairs, where Rose keeps her coal. Luckily, I managed to brush all the coal dust off it. He thought it was a great joke!

Cyril has turned out to be a really great bloke, hasn't he? I wasn't too sure about him at first. He seemed so quiet that I thought our Rose would eat him up, but I'm really impressed with how he handles her. They seem to be truly happy together. Do you think they'll have any more kids, or will Douglas be their only one?

Speaking of kids, my little Dot is thriving. She likes her new school, although she was very disappointed that they wouldn't put her in for the eleven-plus exam. They said she was too late registering or something. Lizzie did go marching down to the school to try and get them to change their minds, but no such luck. They said that because she is such a bright girl she'll do okay without sitting the exam, but I know she's upset over it. She really wanted to get that certificate. Still, never mind that. Apparently, she has her heart set on becoming a seamstress like you, Mum. She is so much like her mother. Though I expect she might change her mind when the time comes, for now, she's adamant. The other options are a poet, an author, an artist, or an explorer!

Little John is such a happy lad. He is smart, but nowhere near as clever as our Dot. Sometimes I think he'd be happy if he could just spend all his time trailing 'round after his step-brothers!

We all love the new house. It's brand new, the end house in a row of twelve all joined together. Apparently, they call it a terrace! It's made of red brick with a little porch at the front. It even has a nice little garden at the back, so I've bought a spade and am going to do a bit of gardening. Lizzie reckons we can even grow our own vegetables. We've already planted an apple tree, although I expect it will take a few years before we get any fruit from it.

Dot has her own bedroom now. It's very small, but there's enough room for her little bed and a chest of drawers. At least she doesn't have to share with the boys anymore, she was getting a bit big to do that. The three boys share the big room at the front, although Tommy doesn't spend much time at home these days. He's either at work or visiting his lady friend. Yes, our boy is courting! A very nice girl he met at work. She lives up Wimbledon way, so he spends a lot of time cycling up there to visit her. Harry is growing up fast too; they're nothing like the little lads I took on when we got married. They were so sweet then, seemed really happy to have a stepdad, but now I'm actually not so sure. We've had a few blow ups recently, silly things like me asking them to put their bikes away properly in the shed rather than just leaving them lying on the lawn and squashing the grass. Of course their mum takes their side, says I'm being unreasonable and that I should leave them alone. I'm sure it's all just a phase. Once they're over this difficult stage I hope it will go back to how it was. Honestly, I'm not sure if this move to the country was the right thing for them. They were older than my two, more established in their London lives. I think they miss all their mates.

Mum, I really do hope you'll manage to pop down and stay with us for a few days soon. You and Olga can share Dot's room, and Lizzie and I have already agreed that Rose and Cyril can have ours. We'll sleep on the settee in the front room. It folds down into a bed so we'll be quite comfy. Then I'll be downstairs already, so it shouldn't disturb any of you when I have to get up early to go to work. I can just hop into the kitchen, have a wash and shave while the kettle's boiling, and then use the toilet without waking anyone. Can you believe we've got an inside toilet now? And a bath. Such luxury!

Anyway Mum, I'd better go now. I've used three sheets of paper to write this. At this rate, the Post Office will charge me more to post it 'cos it's so heavy!

Take care of yourself. Love to you all.

Your loving son,
Valentine

Morden
January 1934

My dearest mother,

I just wanted to say how much we loved having you all here at Christmas, it was such a happy time. Rose and Cyril were so kind to bring all that lovely food. I don't think I've ever felt quite so full up!

We really missed you after you'd gone, the house seemed very quiet.

Lizzie loved the drawings Albert did for us, she's going to frame them and hang them on the wall in the front room. Dot was especially pleased with the one he did of her. He got her likeness so well, that serious look she has on her little face when she's concentrating.

Unfortunately after you'd all left, we had a huge falling out with the boys. Tommy said he and Harry were fed up with me still treating them like kids now that they were both grown up and working. It all blew up a bit. I'm afraid I lost my temper and said some things I probably shouldn't have, and the outcome was that they packed their bags and left. They said they were going back to live in London. Lizzie is distraught, of course, but I keep telling her they'll be back, that she is such a good mum, so indulgent, and they know where their bread is buttered. I must be honest and say that it is quite nice not having them around for a bit. They take up a lot of space and don't really contribute anything. Lizzie is a bit soft and doesn't charge them anything for their keep, so they both tend to indulge themselves with new clothes and outings. Not to mention they've both taken up smoking. I know that Lizzie and I smoke, but we're grown up. They're just kids; I don't think they should be wasting their money on cigarettes. But of course, Lizzie takes their side about that too.

Anyway Mum, enough moaning for now. Look after yourselves. Lots of love to you all, see you soon.

Your loving son,
Valentine

BACK TO THE BEGINNING

My dearest mother,

 My heart is breaking.

 I came home from work at lunchtime two days ago–I hadn't been feeling well, dreadful coughing and spluttering, so the boss sent me home early–and found the house completely empty. All the furniture and everything had gone, even the kid's beds. The only thing left was my Windsor chair. You know, that nice wooden one that Lily's uncle made.

 Lizzie has left me, Mum.

 She pinned a note to the kitchen cupboard saying she was sorry, but she couldn't stay without her boys. Apparently, they told her that they were never coming back.

 She left us the kettle, three plates, three cups, three knives, forks, and spoons, a tin of tea, and a bottle of milk. She's taken everything else–the saucepans, the bowls, the kitchen curtains, everything. She's just left a couple of threadbare towels in the bathroom. I just can't believe it. I thought she was better than this, to just go without saying anything to my face or having a discussion. She never even mentioned having the thought of ending things between us, and certainly never mentioned she was thinking of leaving.

The kids are heartbroken, especially little Dot. She really loved Lizzie, was so happy to have a mother like all her friends. John didn't seem too worried, he was more upset when the two boys stormed off the other week, he looked up to them both so much.

Anyway, we're getting by. We all wept buckets that first night. We didn't have anything to eat and no beds to sleep in, but that nice Mrs. Pratt from next door popped 'round. She'd obviously seen Lizzie drive off with everything in the van (she said that the two boys, Tommy and Harry, came down with Lizzie's dad and helped her with the move) so she brought us 'round some food and blankets and we just slept in the front room, on the bare lino.

Dot wanted to stay at home the next morning, I don't think she wanted to face her friends, who were bound to ask questions. But I told her she needed to go to school because I had to sort things out. I hated sending her, but I had no choice. I don't know how I got through the day really, but my boss was very kind. He gave me a loan to buy some new stuff, so I went to the second hand shop and got three beds, a couple of chairs and a table and some sheets and blankets. Luckily she left the kids clothes and their few bits and pieces, not that they've got much, although Dot has got some pretty little dresses that Lizzie insisted on having made for her. I really thought she loved that girl like she was her own, but I guess I was wrong? I can't believe she's left us, I thought we were happy. I was happy, I really thought she was too.

Oh Mum, I just don't know how we're going to get through this. Dot is heartbroken. Me and her just can't seem to stop crying. John seems happy enough as long as he's got a bit of food in his belly and is allowed to go outside and play with his friends.

Sorry to be so melancholy. I guess I just have to pull up my socks and get on with it. I just wish we'd never left Camden Town. I just wish I'd never married her.

Valentine

MORDEN
1935

Dearest Mother,

I hope this letter finds you all keeping well. I am okay, work-ing hard as usual, but at least now I feel that we are making some headway. It's been such a rough year but I'm glad to say that the kids are doing okay these days. I was so worried about my Dot. She just seemed to fade away after Lizzie left; it hit her so hard. First she loses her own mum, then her step-mum, whom she idolises, just abandons us all.

But I mustn't speak ill of the dead, right? It was such a shock when we got the letter saying Lizzie had died. They didn't say ex-actly what happened, but I think it was probably complications from her heart trouble. When I first met her down in Bognor, the doctors were worried about what her rheumatic disease had done to her heart. I did feel sad when I heard, Mum. I really loved that woman. It was much worse for my little Dot. She must have been bottling up all her feelings, 'cos when I showed her the letter she burst into tears and didn't stop crying for two days. I think maybe 'til that point she had been hoping that Lizzie would come back to us someday. It broke my heart to see her so upset; she's usually such a bright and happy little thing. I was worried it would affect her schoolwork, but if anything, it seems to have made her more determined to succeed. She's still talking about being a seamstress like you and she's due to leave school next year, but I don't think she'll be able to look for a job straight away. I'll need her to stay home and take care of little John while I'm at work. He's too young to stay alone—he would probably forget to turn off the gas after boiling the kettle and blow the whole house up in the process! I worry about him a bit, he's not interested in school at all. He just wants to spend all of his time playing football with his mates! Still, I guess he'll grow up eventually. Dot is wonderful with him, so protective and loving. I think she feels like she has to mother him now. I feel bad about that, she's only 13 after all. She shouldn't be having to deal with all this. She's so good to me, always has my tea ready on the table when I get home from work and my slippers warming by the fire. She's made a nice little home for us. Mrs. Pratt from next door gave her a bit of old material to make some nice curtains and a couple of cushions. Then, she found a bit of dark-green velvet at the church jumble sale and used it to make a big cushion for my Windsor chair. I love that chair. Sometimes after the kids have gone to bed, I sit in it and have a quiet smoke, thinking about everything that's led us here.

I am so grateful to Rose and Cyril for inviting my two to go hop picking with them. They had such a wonderful time, haven't stopped talking about it since they got back! It would have been a long, boring old time for them to have been stuck here alone during the summer holidays while I went to work, so I think having that lovely month in Kent did them both a world of good. I've heard so many stories, they just loved the whole experience and they came back looking like little brown berries. I have sent Rose and Cyril a thank you note, but please say thanks again from me, won't you?

It makes me very happy knowing you are happily settled at Rose's. I would be really worried about you, Albert, and Olga if you were on your own. I know Rose will always take care of you all. Her little Douglas seems like a nice boy; Dot was telling me how kind he was to them down in Kent, always including them in everything and introducing them to his little friends.

Well, I don't have much more news at the minute, so I will close now. I'm looking forward to seeing you all soon. I will probably try to bring the kids up to see you next weekend, we wouldn't mind some of your nice egg and cress sandwiches! And tell Rose not to forget to buy plenty of cakes!

Your loving son,
Valentine

Morden
December 1936

Hello Mum,

I do hope this letter finds you all keeping well. Sorry we haven't been up to see you for a while, things have just been a bit hectic here.

Dot has now left school. She didn't want to really, but we couldn't afford for her to stay on. Her dream was to go on to art school, or even university, but she now realises that people like us can't do those things. I think some of the girls at her school come from rich families, so maybe that's where she got the idea a while back? Anyway, she says she is happy to train as a tailoress instead, if I can manage to find her a position. The only trouble is that she's left-handed, so I don't know if I'm going to be able to get anyone willing to take her on. I am going to start chatting to all the little workshops I collect stuff from, maybe one of them will be able to help? In the meantime, she's doing a good job keeping the house going and looking after John while he finishes his last few months at school. He doesn't have any ambition or any idea of what he wants to do. I'm hoping he might find a job locally.

What a year this is turning out to be! First losing the old king, then hearing that the Prince of Wales abdicated so he could marry that American woman. Such a turnup for the books with Jesse Owens winning all those gold medals at the Summer Olympics... I doubt Adolf Hitler was too pleased about that. He's always so vocal about Germans being superior. Along with that, I'm a bit worried about this Spanish Civil War. I hope too many young men don't lose their lives like they did in 1918.

Can you believe that the Crystal Palace has been burned down to the ground? Apparently, there were at least 80 fire engines there trying to put out the blaze. I know it had been in disrepair for years, but it's still such a shame. Another bit of our history, gone.

Talking of history, I hear some sorry tales these days. Lots of people who've fled from Germany and Holland, trying to escape from the Nazis. I guess they sense bad things are coming. Some of them are really struggling to make ends meet. My heart breaks for them; it must be so hard to feel you have to leave the country of your birth just to survive. I met an old Dutch chap last week who was roaming the streets looking for work. He asked me if I wanted to buy one of his treasures, one of the few valuable things he'd managed to bring with him to London. I felt sorry for him so I paid him 35 pounds, probably more than it's worth honestly. That's okay. When I brought it home Dot said she loved it, asked if she could have it and said she would pay me back when she started work! You know I can't refuse that girl anything. She is such a lovely child and has kept this family together since Lizzie left. Anyway, she has it now, it has pride of place on her chest of drawers. It's a nice thing, made of solid silver and in the shape of a mandolin.

Looking forward to seeing you all for Christmas. It will be good to spend the holiday together at Rose's place. The kids and I are really looking forward to it.

Take care 'til then.

Your loving son,
Valentine

January 1937

Dear Rose,

Just a quick line to say thanks again for such a great Christmas. It was so good for the kids to spend the holiday with all of you. Sometimes I think I've done the wrong thing staying down here in Morden without Lizzie and her boys, maybe I should have just upped sticks and come back to Camden to be with you all.

I guess I just wasn't thinking straight for the first year or so, and now I wonder if it's too late to uproot them again. John seems so happy here, especially as he's going to leave school this year. He just can't wait to get out there into the big world and earn his living. I worry that he's still not very ambitious; he doesn't seem to realise that passing a few exams would get him a better job. Most of his mates are talking about working at the railway depot or the new dairy plant. He's a smart boy and could do so much better, but if I try to reason with him he just stomps off in a huff. I don't think we were that stroppy when we were youngsters, were we Sis? Not sure Mum would have let us get away with it if we'd behaved like that! How's your little Douglas doing? I really enjoyed talking to him at Christmas, he's such a clever little lad. He was telling me he's really good at mathematics and wants to be an engineer. I daresay he will achieve it, too!

Did you manage to chat with our Dot much over the holidays? I do worry sometimes that she hasn't got any female company. She does have a nice friend called Rosie, but apart from her, I worry that Dot gets lonely being home all day by herself. Mind you, she reads a lot; she is always popping down to the library and borrowing a pile of books. I had a glance at the latest one she picked up today by some author called Agatha Christie. It's called the A.B.C. Murders–her head was stuck in it all evening! I could barely get a word out of her. She's been doing a bit of drawing and writing poetry lately too. I have to say, my girl is pretty talented. Despite being left-handed, she writes a fine copperplate hand, says she learnt from watching me... can you believe it! I do worry that I have done her a great disservice by taking her out of school so young though, I really think if circumstances had been different she could have gone on to do great things. Lizzie always reckoned that Dot was the smartest one of us all.

Anyway, talking of writing, can you give Mum a message for me? She seems to think I am wasting lots of money on writing paper for my letters and on drawing paper for Dot. In fact, I get it really cheap. There is a commercial stationers shop in the arcade at the Tube entrance. One day last year I noticed a sign in the window advertising cheap paper. Apparently their machine sometimes cuts it wrong and they can't sell the misshapen bits to their usual customers, so I buy a big pile of it every now and then and Dot and I can scribble to our hearts' content! You know how I've always liked writing letters. Now that I live so far away from you all, it's the best way for me to let you know all our news. Maybe one day we'll get one of those newfangled telephones and I'll have to ring you once a week instead!

I must say, I was a bit worried about Olga when we were visiting for Christmas. She seems to be fading a bit. Now that she has such trouble hearing, it's hard to hold a conversation with her. She's getting on a bit now so I suppose we shouldn't be surprised, but she's been in our lives for as long as I can remember.

I can't imagine her not being around anymore. I think she's been pretty disturbed by all the stuff going on in Russia lately. That chap Stalin seems pretty ruthless, and I guess it must remind her of the life she escaped from all those years ago. Anyway, enough about world affairs. This was just meant to be a quick thank-you note, but as you know, I am not one to keep my thoughts to myself!

Take care of yourself, Rose. Much love to you, Cyril, little Douglas, Mum, Olga, and Albert. I am so glad you're all together, looking out for each other.

Your loving brother,
Valentine

Morden

August 1937

Dearest Mother,

Hope this finds you all keeping well. I know how worried you've been about Olga, hopefully this bit of sunshine we're hav-ing lately will put a bit of colour in her cheeks. I know you two like to have a stroll 'round the park every day, and at least for the last couple of weeks it's stopped raining.

I was thinking of taking a little trip up to Southend before the weather gets too chilly. It would be nice to have a bit of sea air. Maybe you fancy coming with me? We could stay in that little boarding house again, the one we went to with Rose, Cyril, and the kids. I know the food there wasn't up to much, but that doesn't really matter because it's more fun to go out for fish and chips anyway. We could even do away with the dismal old breakfasts at the B&B and go to that nice little café off the seafront. They do a good fry up of sausage, bacon, eggs, and fried bread. It's making my tummy rumble just thinking about it! Anyway, give it some thought, Mum. You can let me know when I pop up to see you this weekend. It wouldn't cost too much, just our train fare and a few bob for food and entertainment. The rooms at the B&B are pretty cheap, mind you, the woman who owns the place is such an old battle axe that people would probably refuse to pay any more!

Do you remember how scared my Dot was when I made us all walk out at low tide to see the wreck of that old German war ship? She was always worried the tide would come back in too soon, before we got back to the beach, and we'd all be drowned. She was always such a little worrier.

What a funny year it's been so far. The Coronation was grand of course. It made you really proud to be English, standing in the Mall with all the crowds and cheering as our new king and queen drove past in their gold carriage. I felt a bit sorry for them though; he never wanted to be the king. I don't think either of them will ever forgive that Wallis Simpson.

In other news, thank goodness all the bus drivers are back at work now. That strike caused a heck of a lot of trouble. At least I could still get to work on the Tube.

What do you think about Neville Chamberlain taking over from Baldwin as Prime Minister? Guess we've got to give him a chance to prove himself.

Did you read that desertion now counts as grounds for divorce? Guess if Lizzie hadn't died, I might have had to use that. Mind you, I can't see myself ever getting married again. The kids don't need another mum now that they're all grown up, and I certainly don't need another woman breaking my heart. There is a young widow up the road who's got two little ones. She always smiles and chats when I walk past her gate on my way home. She seems pleasant enough, but I might have to start walking home the other way. I don't want her to get any ideas!

The kids are doing all right these days. John has left school now—he couldn't wait—and has got himself a job at the new Express Dairies bottling plant. A lot of his mates have gone there too. He's happy because he earns a bit of money and can just cycle there every day. I think he could have done better, could have got a job up in town and travelled on the Tube every day like me, but he said he didn't want to.

Dot on the other hand, can't wait to start her work in town. I am so grateful to Cyril for putting in a good word for her. I really didn't think anyone would take her—you never hear of left-handed tailors—but she starts next week on Berwick Street at a little sitting owned by a chap Cyril knows. She's also so happy that our Rose took her shopping for a new coat to use when she goes into work. It's a bit big, but it was cheap in the sales and will keep her nice and warm on those chilly winter mornings. She'll travel up with me for the first week or so until she gets the hang of it. She's such a wee little thing Mum, I do worry about her trailing around Soho all on her own. Of course that's where most of the tailors' workshops are, not on Saville Row or Bond Street. If those rich old blokes realised their suits were hand-sewn by people in hovels, I bet they'd want them even cheaper. They have no idea how the other half live, how hard most of us have to work for our money.

Anyway, better finish up now before I get too het up about this. It does make my blood boil though, how some of these rich young men who've never done an honest day's work in their lives look down on other people.

I think Dot and I might call in next week on Friday after work so she can tell you how she got on. Put the kettle on at about six o'clock! Looking forward to seeing you all then.

Take care of yourself Mum. Love to you all.

Valentine

Morden
September 1938

My dearest mother,

I do hope you are all keeping well. Glad to hear that Olga is improving. She looked really poorly last time I called in, I thought she was on her last legs. It's good to hear she's rallied a bit.

What do you think of all this latest news? It's all a bit worrying, isn't it? While it's all very well for old Chamberlain to say that the government "emphatically disapproves of what Germany is up to in Austria," it's not looking good when they've started issuing us all with gas masks.

I think Winston Churchill is right when he says there will be trouble if Czechoslovakia is partitioned.

That speech Chamberlain made about the Munich Agreement and "Peace for Our Time" worries me. I overhear lots of the Naval bigwigs who come to Saville Row for their uniform fittings. They all say another war is inevitable. Oh Mum, surely we haven't got to go through all that again... more young men killed like they were last time. They always said that was the "war to end wars."

*I'm so worried about Dot and John if there is another war. They are both old enough to be called up now. Did you know that Rose gave Dot a copy of some fancy new book by Bernard Shaw called **The Intelligent Woman's Guide to Socialism and Capitalism**? Dot has been reading it every morning on the Tube and is constantly spouting bits of it. She seems quite excited about the idea of being called up if we do go to war; she reckons that women are equal to men and can do anything if they're given the chance.*

*Did you hear that old Bertram Mills has died? I used to love taking the kids to his circus when they were young. And J.M. Barrie, who wrote **Peter Pan and Wendy**. I used to read that book, as well as **The Water Babies**, to Dot and John all the time when they were little. One of my bosses at Gieves gave me signed copies of both those books as a present. I think J.M. Barrie was a family friend of theirs or something and he knew my kids would enjoy the stories. Dot still has both of them on the shelf in her bedroom, she treasures them.*

Life is changing so fast Mum, and I'm not sure it's for the best. I expect our Albert is as worried about the prospect of war as I am. We both know how awful it was last time.

Will try to pop in and see you after work one day this week. Just expect me when you see me!

Your loving son,
Valentine

CAMDEN
LONDON
1939

Camden
September 6th, 1939

Dear Valentine,

Sorry I don't write letters to you much, brother. Well actually, hardly at all, but I couldn't let today pass without penning a few lines to you.

Can you believe it's happening again? After all we went through last time?

Germany invaded Poland and Chamberlain really thought Hitler would listen to him and back off? The man is so naïve. Of course Hitler was going to ignore him, and so now we find ourselves at war again.

I am in despair. All those young men going off to be cannon fodder, like we were.

I spent most of yesterday in tears, looking at the place my arm used to be and thinking of how many others are now going to suffer the way I did. Or worse. Oh Valentine, it's all so senseless.

And you must be so worried about your Dot and John. They're safe at the moment, but I don't suppose it will be long before they get called up.

Try to keep your chin up, dear brother. Maybe it won't be as bad as last time.

Your loving brother,
Albert

Camden
October 1940

Dear Son,

I am very sorry to have to tell you that our beloved Olga passed away this morning. We managed to keep her at home right 'til the end, so at least she died as she wanted–in her own bed. She was peaceful at the end, free from all the pain she had been suffering the last few years.

Oh Son, I miss her more than I can tell you. She had been my friend for so many years; in some ways she was like a second mum to me, always there, always looking out for me. We've grown old together and somehow I thought she would always be there at my side. I never imagined having to carry on without her. We had such marvellous times, Valentine, all those years of sewing and running our little business. I remember how kind she was when I was young and we all lived in the slums. And then, when we came back to London after your dad died, she was a life saver. She found us somewhere to live and let me help her with the sewing. I don't think we would have survived that awful time if it hadn't been for her kindness.

Oh Son, how am I going to carry on without her?

Rose and Cyril are very good to me of course, but I don't think they really know what to say. Our Albert is in a world of his own right now, he seems very troubled these days. I think this war is getting the best of him, bringing back too many awful memories.

And of course, this damn Blitz is incredibly frightening. Everyone is so fearful, not knowing if any given day is going to be their last. I dread going outside every morning, never knowing if we'll find the house still standing. Cyril makes sure all our blackout requirements are in place at night and he insists on us going into the Anderson shelter in the garden as soon as we've had our tea. He is such a worrier, but I know he just wants to keep us all safe. Sometimes our Albert refuses to go in there even after the sirens have gone. He seems to have gotten worse since France surrendered. I think it all just brings him to a terribly dark place. Sometimes I wonder if the English Channel is going to be enough to keep Hitler at bay. He's already invaded the Channel Islands.

I do worry about you Valentine, being stuck in the thick of it. Why on earth did you volunteer to be an ARP warden? Every time I hear the sirens I think of you, risking your life just to protect some damned old buildings. In my heart I know you are doing a fine thing though, helping people get to the shelters and putting out the fires.

And I am so very worried about Dot and John. There is talk that everyone over the age of 18 is going to be called up soon. It just breaks my heart thinking of what might happen to them. At least if they were still little we could have them evacuated out to the country, well out of harm's way.

I'm sorry, this letter has turned into a really miserable bit of moaning, but I know you'll understand how I am feeling. This is such a rotten time for everyone, and in some ways, I'm glad Olga isn't going to see any more of it. I don't think the worst is over yet, do you? Stay safe, Valentine.

Your loving mother,
Martha

Morden
Autumn 1941

Dearest Mother and Albert,
What a dreadful time this is. I really thought it would never happen again after the horrendous time we all had in 1914, but I was wrong. I think it's worse this time.

I'm still doing my ARP duties, which of course keeps me up in town most nights. I think everyone's getting pretty fed up now. This war is dragging on so long, there's not much food around and so many people have lost their homes. That Blitz took the stuffing out of all of us, I think. I've seen some pretty sad sights, like little kids sitting in the rubble of their homes, crying 'cos their mum and baby brother were underneath, buried. I saw a little girl sitting perched on all the bricks and rubble from a bookshop that had taken a direct hit. There were still a few fires smouldering there, so I went over to move her on and realised she was reading a book, one she'd found amongst all the debris. She said she'd never been able to afford a book before. It broke my heart. All of this misery, and for what?

Still, at least we're all alive still and hopefully I can pop up and see you all soon. Just not quite sure when exactly as we've lost some of the other wardens–killed on duty. It shook us all up a bit I can tell you, to lose our mates like that. So now I'm on duty five or six nights every week. I don't mind though, someone's got to do it.

Mind you, I'm glad none of us were at home in Morden the other week, as a stray bomb that had come down in the field next door suddenly went off, destroying the house opposite. Our place was okay–thank God–although the event did leave some huge cracks in all the walls and a big chunk of masonry fell right onto Dot's bed. It would probably have killed her if she'd been sleeping there. Luckily, the kids were both away. John was staying at his new girlfriend's place in Tooting and Dot was working a night shift at the food factory in Raynes Park where she and the other girls have been sent while they're waiting for their call up papers. She's pretty fed up; she hates the factory job and would much rather still be doing her tailoring. However, the government has said it's all hands to the wheel and we must all do our bit for the war effort. She's signed up for the ATS–not sure what she'll be doing exactly, but I guess we'll find out soon enough. At least they're not sending women out to the battlefields yet.

Speaking of, John has signed up for the Royal Navy. Oh Mum, it breaks my heart. He and his mates are so excited, just like we were back in 1914 when it all seemed like such a big adventure. They think it's all going to be so easy, wearing their smart sailor uniforms, destroying Hitler and his gang of thugs.

I will let you know as soon as I have more news, but in the meantime Mum, try to keep your chin up. Albert, you make sure you look after Mum and Rose, you lot are very special and precious to me.

With all my love,
Valentine

Morden
1942

Dearest Mother,

I am sorry to say that what we feared has happened. My two lovely kids have been sent off to fight in this damn war.

John is serving in the Royal Navy on a minesweeper somewhere. He was happy to go, but I am worried sick. Every day I listen to the news and hope I don't hear anything bad.

My little Dot is now a soldier. They were all sent up to York for their initial training and the day after they got there, York Railway Station was bombed. Apparently she and the other girls joked that Hitler was determined to get them somehow—even chasing them all the way from London to try to finish them off— but oh Mum, my heart is breaking. I just can't bear the thought of either one of them getting killed.

How is our Albert doing? Are you managing to get him to go into the shelter in the garden now? If not, perhaps you should think about taking him to one of the Tube shelters. They have turned into quite jolly places. Everyone is frightened of course, but somehow down there, in the underground stations, everyone is equal. People share their food, look after each other's kids, and there's often a bit of a singsong going on. He would probably enjoy the company. There's lots of old soldiers down there. I would feel much happier knowing he was safely down there, rather than hiding under the table in the kitchen. At least the Yanks are fighting with us now, although I don't suppose they would have joined in if it weren't for the Pearl Harbor attack. But such bad news about the surrender of Singapore to the Japs. So many of our boys, taken as prisoners of war. I do hope they don't have too bad a time and that this can all be over soon.

Try to take care of yourselves. I worry about you all, but feel better knowing you are with Rose and Cyril. God Bless for now, 'til I see you again.

Your loving son,
Valentine

London
June 1943

Dear Rose,

I thought I would drop you a line about this, and you can decide whether or not to tell Mum.

I have just heard that my little Dot has been sent to work on a searchlight site. Apparently most of these sites are being run by women now, as all the blokes have gone to the frontlines. I am so worried about her, Rose. These sites are in remote fields in the middle of nowhere and that makes them so vulnerable to enemy fire. She seems quite happy, though. Of course, it's her first time away from home apart from the time she went hop picking with you, so I guess it seems like a big adventure. Yesterday I was talking to some army bigwig I delivered a suit to and mentioned that my daughter was in the army on a searchlight site. Guess what he said? "Oh dear, that's not so good. Those girls have to handle all that heavy machinery, dangerous work with the Jerry's flying over every five minutes. And of course, the army won't let the women have guns. But I'm sure your girl will be okay, old chap." That did nothing to ease my anxiety.

Haven't heard anything much from John. I got a standard Navy-approved postcard saying he was all right, but no more information of course. I've no idea where he is; I just hope and pray he stays safe too.

Anyway, I didn't want to worry Mum, that's why I'm writing to you. Please do tell her if you think she should know.

How is Albert doing? Is he managing to do any sketching?

I'm staying up in town most nights now. They need me to do lots of night shifts, and anyway, with the kids gone it's a bit lonely at home. I'll try and pop over and see you all one evening next week.

Take care of yourselves 'til then and try to keep your chins up. This war can't go on forever.

Your loving brother,
Valentine

London 1944

Dearest Mum, Rose, and Albert,

I do hope this finds you all keeping well. What a worry these last few months have been.

These new toys of Hitler's are causing so much damage. Since the doodlebug raids started, there has been so much carnage. Every day more destruction and so much death—mostly civilians. I'm not sure how much more of this we Londoners can stand. This war seems never-ending. I guess this is how it was for Mum and Rose back in 1914, when we boys were away.

Dot came home on leave last week. She looks really great. All that sunshine and being outside every day has brought her freckles out. She seems very happy, has made some nice friends. She says that having just women on the site has made them all much tougher. She's learnt how to fix engines and everything!

I hated it when she had to go back. However brave she is, it's still jolly dangerous work.

I still don't hear much from John. Dot says it's because he's probably too busy with a girl in every port!

Will try to pop in and see you on Saturday. Lots of love for now.

Valentine

P.S., Marvellous news. Just heard on the radio that Paris has been liberated! Maybe this damn war is on the way out at last!

Camden 1945

My dearest son Valentine,

I can hardly believe it. The war is over at last.

But at what cost? Six years of our lives and millions dead. I am so grateful that we've all survived this terrible time, but my heart broke when I saw the footage of all those poor souls rescued from the concentration camps. All over the world, mothers are grieving for their dead sons and daughters–and for what? What has been achieved by all these years of carnage and heartache?

They say that Adolf Hitler and his cronies have committed suicide. Just shows them up for the cowards they are. They knew they would have to answer for their war crimes if they stayed alive.

At least we are all okay, although I think poor Albert's mind is much more muddled now than it was before the war. Every time he hears a bang–even a door slamming shut–he jumps out of his skin. Rose has decided that we should move to the country, so she and Cyril have bought a house in Edgware. Oh Valentine, I'm not really sure I want to go. I've lived all my life in London, I'm used to it. But I suppose I don't have a choice, right? They have been so good to me all these years. And as Rose said, now that I'm an old lady, I should be content just sitting by the fire and doing my knitting. I think she's joking–you know I've never been much of a knitter! However, I suppose I am old now. I was 74 last birthday, so I've already passed my three score years and ten. But you know Son, inside I still feel young. I get such a shock when I look in the mirror and see an old lady staring back at me!

Anyway, I'm glad we can begin to get on with our lives now that this war's done. Hopefully your Dot and John will be de-mobbed soon, I just can't wait to see them both. I'm glad too that you don't have to do all that ARP stuff anymore, I was terrified at the thought of you patrolling the streets every night.

Take care of yourself, Valentine. Looking forward to seeing you as soon as you can manage a visit. Will let you know when we are moving to Edgware.

Your loving mother,
Martha

MORDEN
1946

Morden 1946

Hello Granny Martha,

I am so glad your move to Edgware went all right. Dad has just been telling me all about it. I arrived home last night and it's so good to be sleeping in my own bed at last! Mind you, I miss all the girls I was on site with, we got really close working in such dangerous conditions. I'm not sure how we're all going to adapt to our lives back in Civvy Street. It feels strange already.

I have got my old job back, working at the tailor's shop on Beak Street. It will seem really funny going back there now that I'm a grown up woman and not just a frightened little girl. When I look back I'm quite proud of how I coped—it was so hard walking into that all-male environment as a naïve 15-year-old. Now it should be a piece of cake. Apparently they even saved my silver thimble, hoping I would come back!

I can't wait to see you all. Dad and I thought we might pop up after work on Friday, we can just get the Northern line Underground right to Edgware. Is it okay if we stay the night? We've got so much to catch up on.

Please give my love to Aunty Rose, Uncle Cyril, and Uncle Albert. Tell Albert he'd better get the pencils sharpened so we can do a bit of drawing together!

With all my love,
Dot

Morden 1946

Dearest Rose,

Thank you so much for a lovely weekend. Dot and I had such a great time, she didn't stop talking about it all the way home. It's wonderful to have her back, I missed her terribly.

I was so happy to see the way our Albert perked up when she arrived. It was almost like he was his old self again. She brought a few of her sketches home—she really is very talented you know, I feel guilty that she never got the chance to realise her dreams. But she seems happy enough for now.

I never told you this before, but I think there was a chap a few years ago whom she was in love with. His name was Bert and she used to mention him a lot in her letters. I think they met at a dance or something. Then one time, last year, she came home on leave looking very pale and wan. She said she was fine, but I was worried, so I kept questioning her. It turned out that Bert had been killed in France. I do worry about her, Rose, she is such a loving girl. I just hope one day she finds another nice chap who sweeps her off her feet. She's only 25, so there's still plenty of time.

I'm not at all worried about our John falling in love, he seems to do that with a different girl every week! I think he woos them with tales of his colourful past as a handsome sailor who's seen the world. Hopefully he'll settle down one day, I wouldn't mind a few grandchildren!

How's your Douglas doing? Guess he's finished at college now? How many more years before he becomes an engineer? Can you believe how well our kids have done, Rose? It is unbelievable when you think how tough our lives were in comparison, growing up in the slums of the East End. What a long way we've all come, me with my council house in Morden and you in that posh Tudor Style detached house in Edgware!

In other news, this rationing has us all in a bit of a bind, doesn't it? I can't wait for the day we can eat as much food as we'd like!

We enjoyed watching the television when we came up to your place. So good that the BBC has started broadcasting again. I think now that Dot and John are both home and working again, we might save up and buy ourselves a little set. Mrs. Pratt next door has got one now, so sometimes Dot pops 'round there and watches it. She enjoys spending time with Mrs. P's grandchildren. She's got four now, and apparently her smallest grandson loves the Muffin the Mule programme. Honestly, I think our Dot does too!

Anyway, I'd better close now, not much going on at present. Lots of love to you all. Tell that brother of ours to keep up the sketching! Thanks for taking such good care of Mum, that country air in Edgware seems to really agree with her. She looks better than ever!

Your loving brother,
Valentine

Edgware 1947

Dear Valentine,

Thanks for your last letter, I'm sorry it's taken me so long to reply.

Sorry we couldn't make it down at Christmas, but as you know, we had to make that emergency trip to Norfolk to see Cyril's dying father. I'm not sure why we had to go, since his family cut him off when he married me, but you know my Cyril. He's a gentleman with a heart of gold. So we traipsed up there, took about six hours in the car as we had to keep stopping to put water in the radiator! When we finally arrived I couldn't believe my eyes. It looked like a stately home, with a butler and every-thing! His Mother was pretty frosty but his dad, poor in health as he was, was a real gent. He kissed my hand and told me how sorry he was that he'd never met me before and how he regretted it, knowing I'd made Cyril so happy all these years. Then he dropped dead the next day and Cyril's mum couldn't wait to get rid of us. I met his brother as well, a stuck-up, unpleasant piece of goods he was—the type who pretends they're holier than thou when in reality they're cheating on their wives and getting all the housemaids pregnant. He was obviously worried that if we stayed too long, Cyril might want to fight for his inheritance! Just shows how little he knows his brother; my husband is an honourable man.

Anyway, I understand that Mum and Albert had a lovely time staying with you. We've heard so many stories. It probably did them both good to have a change of scene, they are both happy living with us (I think!) but I know they miss Camden. Sometimes I feel really guilty about dragging them out here.

In other news, I'm glad to know that Dot and John are both working and able to help you a bit with all the bills. Mum said you were even thinking of buying a television! I think that's a grand idea, we love ours.

What do you think about all this talk of a Cold War? It's a bit of a worry; I thought we were done with wars after going through the last one. Cyril brings me home a couple of papers every night: the Times and the Daily Mail, that way I get a balanced view of everything. And of course, the Mail has a great sporting section. Do you still do the football pools? I do it every single week, Cyril laughs at me, says it's a mug's game, but I always think it might be my lucky week. You know how I've always liked a bit of a gamble! Talking of which, shall we go to the Epsom Derby again this year? We could go on the charabanc with Cyril's work so we'd be parked right on the Downs, directly in front of the grandstand. Might even see the old king and queen in their box there! It was so exciting to be there last year, wasn't it? It made us forget a little about all the war years when it was cancelled. Do you remember how excited I got when my horse, Airborne, won? You all thought I was mad betting on an outsider like that, but you had to eat your words when I collected my winnings! Anyway Valentine, do say you'll come, Dot and John too if they fancy it. We'll have a grand day out. I always like having my fortune read by the old gypsy, Rosie Lee there, and of course there's all those fairground attractions too. The kids used to love those when they were little. I don't suppose our Douglas will come, he seems to think all that's a bit beneath him. I'm sorry to say he's become a bit of a snob since he went to that smart college. I overheard him talking to some of his new mates, boasting about his dad's family estate in Norfolk. Don't suppose he mentions my humble upbringing in the East End!

What do you think about all these countries getting their independence? India and Pakistan, and now the State of Israel being established! And what about the nationalisation of the coal mines? I think that will be good, as long as it provides better conditions for the miners.

Anyway Valentine, I must close now. Mum is calling for a cup of tea, so I'd better jump to it!

Do come and see us anytime you can. The kettle will always be on. By the way, did I tell you I've been growing gooseberries and have a really good crop this year? Bet you never thought your old sister would become a gardener!

With love from us all,
Your sister Rose

Morden, 1948

Dear Rose,

This is just a very quick note scribbled in haste on the train!

Can you believe they've established a National Health Service at last? We can all, rich and poor alike, now get free medical care! What a marvellous thing that is. Just imagine how many lives are going to be saved—especially among the poor (like we used to be) who can't afford to pay for a doctor.

I am very happy to think that our children and grandchildren will be better cared for than we ever were.

Much love to you all. Please give Mum and Albert (and of course Cyril and Douglas) a hug from me.
God Bless.

Your brother,
Valentine

Morden
1949

Dearest Mother,

I am so happy to hear from Rose that you are getting better after your fall. She said you were standing on a ladder, trying to pick apples from the tree in the garden when you stretched too far and slipped off. Lucky you only twisted your ankle and got a few bruises—it could have been much worse. Mum, you're getting a bit old for all this! After all, you'll be 80 in a couple of years and we really want you around a bit longer. Anyway, you've got to take care of yourself because you've got a couple of weddings to go to… Yes, both my kids have announced that they're getting married!

Dot has met a nice young man through a mutual friend. His name is Ben and he's a smart lad, an electronics engineer. He was in the Royal Air Force and spent the war years in South Africa, fixing planes. He's an only child whose parents live up the road at Rosehill. They seem nice enough, real Cockneys, who moved there from Southwark when Ben was a little lad. Like us, they were relocated from London during the slum clearances.

John's lady is called Jean. She's a bit older than he is and reminds me a lot of that Wallis Simpson. She seems a bit hard, but my boy seems besotted with her and has bought her a nice ring.

Dot was planning to get married in July, but John and Jean stole her thunder and announced that they were planning a July wedding. Of course my Dot, being the gentle, kind-hearted soul she is, backed down and said they could have July and she'd re-arrange hers for next March. I think she's a bit disappointed, but is putting on a brave face for her brother's sake. She has always put that boy first and sometimes I think he takes advantage of her good nature.

So, anyway Mum, I think Dot is planning a little shopping trip with you and Rose in the next couple of weeks. Apparently she is planning to buy the material and make her own dress, so I am sure it will be beautiful. She has turned out to be such a good tailor. How I wish her mum was still around to see her. Lily would be so proud of how our little girl has turned out.

*Take care of yourself, Mum, no more tree climbing please!
See you soon.*

*Your loving son,
Valentine*

Morden 1950

Dearest Mother,

*What a wonderful year we've had. Two weddings and now
a granddaughter.*

*I think Jean must have already been expecting when she
and John got married—maybe that's why she was so adamant
about wanting a July wedding. Anyway, none of that matters
now, little baby Sarah has arrived safe and sound and already,
she's the apple of my eye. Hopefully Dot will get pregnant soon
as well, although if you remember there is a bit of doubt about
whether she'll be able to have a baby of her own after all that
illness she had when she was small. I think she and Ben are
considering adoption; she mentioned that they'd paid a visit
last weekend to a children's home. I watched her when she was
cuddling baby Sarah and she looked so sad. She would make a
marvellous mother.*

*Things have gone a bit pear-shaped accommodation-wise. As
you know, there's a real shortage of housing for all these young
married ones, so most of them are having to stay with family. I
always assumed Dot and Ben would come to me, we get on so
well and it would have been a happy household. Sadly though,
that Jean got in first and insisted that she and John should move*

in here instead. Before I could even discuss it with Dot, they were installed in the big front bedroom and said that the baby could have Dot's room when she moved out! Of course my lovely girl didn't argue, didn't fight her corner, just smiled and moved to her in-laws' at Rosehill. I am worried about her, Mum. I don't think she really feels comfortable there. I probably should have stood up for her more. But my new daughter-in-law has a sharp tongue.

Anyway, I'm looking forward to seeing you this weekend. Dot and Ben have agreed to come up with me, so we'll stay on Friday and Saturday nights if that's okay. I know Rose won't mind, she always enjoys our company.

See you then.

Your loving son,
Valentine

Morden 1952

Dearest Mother,

I am so thrilled to tell you that I am a grandfather again. My little Dot finally managed to have a baby; you know how much she went through during her pregnancy. It was always a bit touch-and-go on whether she'd be able to keep the baby. She was very poorly at times, that's why we didn't broadcast the news about her expecting. Anyway, all was well in the end and she has a dear little baby girl they are calling Ann. When I first saw her it gave me quite a shock; she looks very much like our Rose. If the baby has the same kind of temperament as my Dot, she will do well in life. I have never seen my girl smile so much, she was born to be a mother. I am just really sad that my Lily isn't here to see our little family grow. I would have also enjoyed it if Lizzie were still around—I forgave her years ago—as I do think at a time like this a girl needs some female support. Dot and Jean aren't really close, I think Jean wants my boy all to herself. And unfortunately, Dot and her mother-in-law don't always see eye to eye. I don't think the old girl would consider anyone good enough for her son! I just wish Dot was still living here with me, then I could keep a proper eye on her. But John's wife has got her feet under the table now and I can't see her shifting one bit!

Anyway, enough moaning. Congratulate me on being a grandfather twice over! I think it's marvellous.

With love,
Valentine

EDGWARE
1953

Edgware 1953

Dear Valentine

I have some very sad news. It's not about Mum—she's okay—even though she's getting a bit doddery these days.

It's our Albert. He fell onto the lighted fire in the front room, just tripped up on the rug and lost his balance. Mum was having a nap upstairs and I was working out in the garden when I heard him screaming. I rushed in and managed to pick him up, but he's very badly burned. The ambulance came very quickly and he's stable in hospital, but I think you should come as soon as you can. Maybe Dot would like to come too, she's always been so fond of him.

Will let you know if there's any change.

With love,
Rose

Edgware

Dearest Valentine,

I was so glad you, Dot, and baby Ann were able to get here in time to see Albert before he passed away. He was so happy to see you all. I will never forget the look on his face as he held baby Ann, the tears were rolling down his cheeks. At least we made him happy in his last few days. He wouldn't have wanted to carry on even if they had managed to do the skin grafts they were talking about. He was always quite vain, checking his appearance in the mirror. I used to tease him and say it was because he was an artist and was constantly looking for perfection. Oh Valentine, I will miss him. Although he was so quiet, he was lovely to have around. Mum is in pieces, another of her babies gone. It seems so unfair for a mother to outlive her children, doesn't it?

I'm glad we could give him a decent funeral. Can you believe how many people turned up for it? I never realised how popular he was. Just a shame most of them never bothered to come and see him much when he was alive. Now it's just you and me left, Valentine, the only two remaining. We must do the best for her that we possibly can. I am really worried she'll go downhill quickly after this, but I might be wrong. She's a tough old bird!

Anyway Valentine, please take care of yourself. You're the only brother I've got now.

Your loving sister,
Rose

Morden
June 1953

Dear Mother and Rose,

Hope this letter finds you both keeping well.

I just had to write to say what a marvellous day we had for the Coronation yesterday. Young Queen Elizabeth did so well, she looked a bit overcome at times but she certainly did us all proud. I wonder if she'll have as good a reign as Queen Elizabeth I... 45 years! Fancy having your whole life planned out for you, it must be a daunting prospect. Anyway, we watched it next door on old Mrs. Pratt's television. We still haven't managed to buy one ourselves, although John tells me you can rent them now so he's going to look into that. She dragged it outside onto the little front lawn so all us neighbours could watch and then we all had a street party, bunting hung from the lampposts, the tables were covered in red, white, and blue cloths, and there was more food than we've seen since rationing began! I wanted to invite Dot, Ben, and little Ann to join us, but Jean wasn't very keen. She said they were bound to be doing something else. I really wish I was better at standing up to her, but somehow she makes me feel like I'm just a stupid old man who doesn't deserve an opinion. And she's living in my house, where I still pay the rent!

Anyway, I'd better stop now before I end up saying too much! Much love to you both. Regards to Cyril and young Douglas.

With love,
Valentine

Morden
February 1955

Dearest Mother and Rose,

Well, I don't think I've ever been so chilly in my entire life! This Big Freeze is certainly something. I've got chilblains from the cold and have been putting my toes so close to the fire, trying to keep my feet warm!

I haven't been able to get to work as the snow has messed up all the rails and there are no trains running. The buses can't get going either, so we're all stuck at home.

I'm finding living with my daughter-in-law a bit tiresome. She's nothing like my Dot. She's not really interested in making a nice cosy home, she just likes to sit around knitting or reading the paper. She is a good cook though, so we're all well fed. I don't think marriage or motherhood is quite what she expected. Like a lot of these young women she just sees the glamorous side of it, doesn't realise you have to work at making a happy marriage. Listen to me! As if I'm in any position to give marriage advice, having had one wife die on me and the other run away. But I do worry that this isn't working out quite like my John hoped. He was pretty young when they got married, and although he'd obviously sowed his wild oats, I don't think he was really prepared for marriage. He is a good loyal boy at heart and it makes me sad that there is not as much affection in it as he would have liked. I think he wanted a few more kids too, but she is adamant that little Sarah is going to be their only one. He looks rather sad at times, but of course there's nothing I can do or say to help him. So I just take myself off to the Crown and have a couple of pints, that way they can have the house to themselves for a while. Mind you, when I do get back nothing's changed. She's still sitting there doing her knitting, smoking away, while John looks after the little one. She's a bonny little girl, although I do think she's a bit spoiled. She has pretty bad tantrums and throws things around when she's angry.

Dot pops in every few weeks to see me, especially if Ben is doing overtime. Her little Ann is a treasure, she's got the same happy gentle disposition as her mum. When the cousins play I always notice that Ann gives in, lets her older cousin be in charge and rule the roost!

Anyway, a bit of good news. My Dot is going to have another baby. She is so thrilled, after all these years thinking she would never be able to have children of her own. I just hope she will manage, I don't think she gets much support from her in-laws, not that she would ever complain.

Well, take care of yourselves and try to stay warm. Spring is on the way!

See you as soon as we can travel again.

With love,
Valentine

MORDEN
1960

Morden

1960

Dearest Mum,

It seems like it's been ages since I saw you last. Life just seems to be so busy, taking away every bit of my energy and never leaving enough time to spend with the people I really care about. But that's all about to change.

Yes, I am going to retire.

I did think about staying on for a couple more years, but the new young bosses at the company made it quite plain that I had overstayed my welcome. They said they would give me a small bonus and a gold watch if I went now, so it seemed like the best option. It was that or hanging on even longer and maybe getting chucked out later anyway!

It's like the end of an era; can you believe how long I've been working here? 26 years. A lifetime. I must say I will be sad to go, I really have enjoyed my time. I've met so many great people, rich and poor, and I've certainly got enough stories to keep all my mates amused when I pop down the pub to while away some of this newfound freedom. Actually, I'm not really sure what I'm going to do with myself now. John and Sarah will be out all day and I don't have much to say to that daughter-in-law of mine. It's hard to live with someone, especially in your own home, when you know they resent your presence and would much rather you were out of the way–preferably permanently! Still, I daresay we'll muddle along. I'll probably have to learn to keep my mouth shut a bit since we don't agree on much. Not to mention, I hate how much she smokes. All the ceilings have gone a horrible brown colour and the house will forever smell like a packet of Senior Service. I know I smoke too, but I only have three or four a day. Meanwhile, she goes through packet after packet. She has got some good qualities, of course, she's not all bad. She's also a great little knitter. Every Christmas we all get something handknitted by her–truly some really nice stuff–but the minute you open the wrapping paper the smell of cigarettes hits you. I know I'm complaining quite a bit, but I actually don't mind the smell too much; I guess I'm used to it now. However, I did notice little Ann's nose wrinkle when she opened her parcel. She recovered quickly–Dot has made sure her girls have good manners–and got up to hug her aunty and say thank you. I noticed she didn't put the cardigan on straight away, though. She probably wanted to wait 'til her mum had washed it to get rid of the smell!

Have you heard they're now talking about smoking being bad for you? Apparently they're saying it causes lung cancer or something? I don't know if that's true, but it's been in all the papers lately.

One bit of good news, just in time for my retirement. We finally got a television set! I'm very pleased about it, especially because I'm going to have so much time on my hands soon. We've been talking about it for ages as you know, just have never quite gotten 'round to saving enough money to buy one outright. Anyway, John heard about a company called Radio Rentals, where you can rent a nice little black and white set for about a pound a week. We signed up and it was delivered last week. It's a great idea, takes away all the worry! If it goes wrong or breaks, they just send someone 'round to fix it. I've realized that I love watching television. I like BBC1, but Jean and Sarah reckon ITV is better. We sometimes have a bit of a heated discussion about what we're going to watch, but John and I usually let the women win. I'm old enough now to know that that's the only way to get a bit of peace and quiet!

Anyway, I've already got some real favourites. I really enjoy Maigret and Scotland Yard (apparently they are drama documentaries of real cases the police have had to deal with— drug smuggling, theft and the like). I'm also enjoying two new programmes. One is called Coronation Street, and it's about a community up North. Mind you, most of the action seems to centre around the pub called the Rovers Return. The other one is called Bootsie and Snudge. That one makes me laugh out loud; all those antics of a couple of old army lads makes me feel young again! The other day we started watching a show called How Green Was My Valley, which is all about the folk in a Welsh mining village. Also, we watch the news every night and on Saturdays it's great for Jean to check off her football results. The only worry I have is that all of this television watching might keep people inside too much. You don't see anyone out and about in the evenings like you used to, people seem to keep to themselves much more these days.

I don't know many people on my street anymore. When we first moved here in the 30s there was much more of a community feel about the place. I guess that was because most of us were from London, glad to be in the country with a bit of space around us. But of course, it's all changing fast. Morden is getting so built up now, nearly all the green fields have gone and I have a devil of a job getting a seat on the Tube every morning. The journey up to town isn't what it used to be, too many people everywhere, everyone in a mad rush all the time... Maybe it's a good thing I'm retiring, I'm beginning to sound like a grumpy old man!

Most of our old neighbours have died or moved on, but old Mrs. Pratt is still next door. Do you know, in all the years we've been neighbours, I've never been inside her house? I've only stood chatting on the front door step or over the garden fence. I don't even know what her real name is, I've always just called her Mrs. Pratt. I also don't think she's that much older than me—maybe by 10 years or so. But I'll never forget how kind she was when Lizzie first left us. She was always popping 'round with bits of food and things, and I know she and Dot used to have the odd cup of tea together while I was at work. I always appreciated her keeping an eye on my girl during that awful time. Anyway, I was doing a bit of gardening the other day, planting some new cabbages, when she called to me over the fence. We stood and chatted for a while which was nice, and she mentioned how well the Virginia creeper was doing. We had a good laugh remembering how excited I was when I first planted it, and then how miserable I was when it didn't do much for the first couple of years. You should see it now Mum, it covers nearly the whole house–right to the upstairs bedroom windows. It's quite magnificent when it goes red in the autumn.

I do wish Lizzie had been here to see it now, she was so excited about having a garden. I've been thinking about her a lot lately. She was a good woman and we really did love each other, but those boys of hers never really accepted me. I suppose it was a bit naïve of me to think I could replace their dad like that. I often wonder how things would be now if she hadn't left. I reckon we would have muddled along quite happily. We did have some lovely times together, we used to laugh all the time and she was so good with my Dot. I feel so guilty that my poor girl only had her own mother for three years, then her step-mum for just a few more. She loved both of them so much. I often wonder if it's done her any harm in the long term. She's a wonderful mother to her lot, but sometimes she does seem rather sad.

It's time for me to close, before I run out of paper and you get fed up reading all my thoughts! I hope you weren't one of those people at that CND rally in Trafalgar Square. They reckon there were more than 20,000 people there; can you believe it? Not a suitable outing for an old lady like you!

See you soon.

Your loving son,
Valentine

EDGWARE
1963

Edgware

1963

My dear son Valentine,

I hope you are all well. I got a nice letter from your Dot the other day telling me about her latest arrival. Three little girls now! I wonder, do you think she was hoping for a boy this time? Anyway, both she and the babe are well, which is the most important thing. She said she had a home birth, apparently she didn't want to go to hospital this time. I don't understand it. All the poor women in my day and for hundreds of years before that would have given anything to give birth in a nice, clean hospital instead of dying in the slums with only a single drunken midwife in tow. But, I guess these young ones must think they know what they're doing. I'd just be worried if something went wrong and they couldn't get to hospital in time.

Oh well, I guess that's just a sign of the changing times, and thankfully all is well with Dot and her new little one. I've lived so long and seen so many changes that nothing much shocks me anymore. I reckon that people just make the same mistakes now as they have done for centuries; no one seems to learn anything from history!

Even as we are blessed to be welcoming new lives into the world as of late, I've also been thinking a lot about the ones who have left us. I do miss Olga terribly still. We used to have such lovely chats about everything, from world affairs to what colour ribbon with which we should trim a dress. And of course, I will always grieve for our Albert. He was a lovely lad and such a talented artist. Rose has a few of his drawings nicely framed and hung, some in my room and some in the front parlour, over the piano. We have all decided that when the time comes, they will be passed down to your Dot. She's the only one who will truly appreciate them.

Do you think Valentine, that when our boy got to heaven his arm was restored? He never really accepted his fate after the war and I just hope he is happy with who he is at last.

To be quite honest, I have been thinking a lot about death lately. It's funny really as I'm fit as a fiddle, but I guess at my age you have to face reality. I can't go on forever, and I have just had my 91st birthday. Mind you, I'm not expecting to go anywhere just yet–Rose and Cyril look after me so well.

Things are so different now than when I was young, Valentine, or even than when you and your sister were children. I'm shocked when Rose takes me out shopping; all these young women seem to have so much freedom. Lots of money to spend on themselves, although you wouldn't think so with some of the rubbish they wear. You hardly ever see anyone in a nicely-cut suit or dress anymore, I think it's all ready-made stuff these days. At the same time, I'm very happy that these young women have so many opportunities to do what they want in life. They don't have to just be content with working some boring, poorly-paid job that they have to give up the minute they get married. And with this new birth pill, they don't even have to rush into having babies if they don't want to. It's all so different, much better I'd say. I just hope they take advantage of their freedom and don't throw it all away. Those suffragettes worked too hard for everything that exists today for it to just be tossed aside by some silly little girls who don't know how lucky they are!

Anyway, enough ranting from me. It's taken me all my energy to sit down and write this letter, I don't do much of this anymore. Therefore, you should feel very honoured that I've bothered to do it for you!

Take care of yourself, Son. I look forward to seeing you as soon as you can manage to pop up here. I know it's a bit far. I'm happy enough in Edgware now, but sometimes I wish we'd never left Camden. I still think of it as my home.

Your loving mother,
Martha

Edgware
1966

Dearest Valentine,

I am so sorry to have to tell you that Mother passed away this afternoon. It truly came as such a shock, since she has seemed so well of late. We had been out for a little drive in the country (you know how she loves an adventure) and when we got home she said she was feeling a bit weary and would go and have a lie down before tea. When I went up there an hour later, she was gone. But oh Valentine, she looked so peaceful, just like she had fallen into a nice, deep sleep. I sat and held her hand for a while, then Cyril called the doctor and the undertakers. She is now in the Chapel of Rest here in Edgware, so when you come up we can go and see her together.

I am so sorry I couldn't tell you straight away, but it has been hectic here and of course you haven't got a phone at home. Cyril says he is happy to drive down and pick you up tomorrow, then you can be here to help me make arrangements for the funeral. Mum bought that plot at Finchley cemetery a few years ago, so at least she'll be near Albert, Lily, and your babies. Olga's buried there too, so Mum will be with her best friend once again.

Oh brother, my heart is breaking. She was the best mum anyone could wish for, wasn't she? We're all going to miss her terribly. I really can't believe she's gone.

Anyway, I must close now. My tears are making the paper all wet, so forgive me if there are any smudges.

Looking forward to seeing you tomorrow. I really need my brother right now.

Your loving sister,
Rose

MORDEN
1968

Morden

March 1968

Dear Rose,

I hope this letter finds you keeping well.

Happy Birthday, Sis. I can't believe you're 78 years old now and your Cyril has just turned 80! When did we ever get to be so old? It only seems five minutes ago that we were all in our twenties and full of hopes and dreams. Even I'm feeling my age a bit these days, now that I'm in my seventies. Seventy-three to be precise!

How is your Cyril doing these days? It has been difficult to see how the stroke has affected his communication and I know it must be so hard for you, Rose. I think the worst thing for him is not being allowed to drive anymore. He always has loved his cars, although I must say I did worry about his driving the last few years; he went a bit too fast for my liking! Do you remember when he got that old motorbike with the sidecar and insisted we all take it in turns to go out for a spin with him? You and I weren't that keen, but do you remember how much Mum loved it? When they got back that first time–after being out for an hour or more–you started telling Cyril off, shouting at him that you'd been worried they'd had an accident? Mum told you off and said she'd been the one who insisted they stay out so long, as she was having such a wonderful time! After that, she used to nag him to take her on little trips quite often. She used to love climbing into that uncomfortable old sidecar, always wearing her flowery headscarf to protect her perm from the wind. She said it was the most fun she'd had in her whole life... And she was in her nineties then!

Oh Rose, I miss her so much. She was the most wonderful mother. She always put us first. I guess we just have to be grateful that she went quickly and without suffering. How lovely to just fall asleep in your own bed after a long, beautiful life, and never wake up again. It was peaceful for her, but awful for us. She'd always been so fit and healthy; I guess we just thought she'd go on forever.

It's funny to think that our kids are probably worried about us dying these days. Life's a silly old business isn't it? One generation making way for the next for all eternity. We all think we're so invincible; I certainly never imagined I'd be this old man sitting in his armchair day after day with nothing much to do. It seems such a long time ago that I felt this house was really my home. Now it's just somewhere I live. During all the time I was getting up every day and going to work, it was okay. It was nice to come back to a hot dinner and some company. But now that I'm retired and home all day, I think I just live my life constantly getting on Jean's nerves. She had been used to having the place to herself all the years I worked, since John Sarah were both gone as well. I feel she resents me being around all the time. I try to give her a bit of space by going out for a walk every day. I wander first down to the shops, then 'round the park. I stay out as long as I can, but of course, these old legs don't work as well as they used to. I have to sit down every now and then. Jean doesn't go out much at all anymore either. It's strange actually, because when they were younger, she was always nagging John to take her out. Now she barely leaves the house, just sits in her chair knitting and smoking. She doesn't even read a book. The only time I see her getting excited is when she's checking the football results on a Saturday afternoon! I do wonder if my John's been happy with her all these years. He's a good boy, very loving and loyal, but sometimes I wonder if he would have liked a different life. Their Sarah is very grown up now. You didn't see her last time you popped in because she was out with her new boyfriend. I'm not too sure about him, he's a bit too smarmy for my taste. Do you know he turned up to take her out wearing blue jeans? She was all done up in a sparkly pink dress looking really pretty, and he wore jeans! Didn't even shake my hand, just gave me a nod. I don't know where these young ones get their manners from.

I know we're not supposed to have favourites, but I do love Dot's eldest girl. Ann popped in here yesterday to visit me on her way home from work. She wanted to show off her new car. She just bought it, an old banger, a Morris 1000. It's her pride and joy. She insisted on taking me for a little spin 'round the block and I must say, she's a good little driver. I felt very safe. She's a hard worker too, she got herself a good job at the bank and seems to be enjoying it as of now.

Oh Rose, she does remind me so much of you. Maybe that's why I'm so fond of her. She's only a tiny little thing as you know, but she's got an enormous and wonderful heart. She cares so much about other people and if you'd seen her the other day, spouting off about apartheid and how everyone in the world should be equal regardless of their class or colour, you'd have been so proud. I wanted to cheer, it was just like listening to you! You two would have made fine suffragettes, the pair of you are so feisty and passionate about these matters. I just hope one day she finds a man worthy of her, although I do worry that with her gentle nature she might get walked over a bit.

Dot's other children are all thriving. They're doing well at school and seem happy. I do worry about my girl, though. Dot has always put such a brave face on about everything. You never really hear her moan, but I think she's probably had a lot to moan about over the years. Ben has been a good husband I think, although only she can say for sure. He's always been there, worked hard to support them all, and is a good father. I think it's been hard for them both. One minute he was a carefree young man, home from the war to be cosseted by his adoring mother, then all of a sudden he was thrusted into marriage and fatherhood before he was really ready. I don't think the move out to the country was right for them, either. I know it wasn't ideal to be living with his mum and dad, especially once baby number two came along, so I understand why a new council house of their own seemed so attractive. But Rose, it's like history repeating itself? Do you remember how Lizzie and I left Battersea to move here? It was for exactly the same reason, to get away from sharing an overcrowded house with in-laws. Look how that ended. I really believe that if we'd stayed in Battersea, Lizzie and I would never have parted. It was too hard for her to be away from her family, from everything she knew. It's for this reason that I worry about my Dot. Sometimes she just looks so pale and unhappy. I feel guilty that I don't go and see her as often as I should. It's only an hour on the bus and then a 20-minute walk to her house, but somehow it seems like a big mission that I can't face doing more than a couple of times a year. I do enjoy my time when I go though; they are all so delighted to see me and I them. It's pretty ironic that I spend all day every day with a daughter-in-law who can't stand me, rather than with my own daughter (who can stand me) and her lovely children. Now that Ann has got her little car, I might see if she can run me over there on occasion.

Well, I seem to have gotten a bit carried away writing this. Sorry it's so long, Rose. If you were nearby I could just say it all to you and not waste so much paper!

I'm going to pop off to the Crown now. I go most days, have a couple half pints of bitter and read the paper. It gets me out of the house for a couple of hours. I used to love chatting to my mates there—sometimes we played cribbage or even had a game of darts—but sadly everyone is dying off. There's only a couple of us old codgers left. That's one of the worst bits about getting old, isn't it? All your old friends are dying around you. It certainly makes you aware of your own mortality. As if looking in the mirror didn't do that enough!

Take care of yourself, Rose. Lots of love to you and Cyril.

Hoping to see you again soon.

Valentine

MORDEN
DECEMBER 28TH, 1968

Valentine George sat in his old Windsor chair, trying desperately to keep his eyes open.

A coal fire was blazing in the hearth and his chair was drawn up close to it, ensuring that his old bones didn't catch cold. The warmth from the fire and the rather soothing orange flames were making him doze off.

It had been such a hectic few days. The whole family had been in his home for Christmas, and as usual it had been a wonderful, happy time. All the people he loved most in the world had been in the little house: his two children and their own children–the little nippers, as he affectionately called them. Rose and Cyril had popped in at teatime on Boxing Day, reluctantly chauffeured by Douglas and his wife, who had made it quite clear that they would much rather be sipping cocktails at the country club.

He smiled as he re-lived Christmas Day in his head, right from the beginning.

He had woken up in the little bedroom where he had slept alone for the last forty or so years.

He sat up in bed, slowly drinking the cup of tea that dear Ann had delivered to him in the hope of getting him up. It was a family tradition that no one could open their presents until he, Grandad, the patriarch of the family, was downstairs, fully dressed and shaved.

From the comfort of his bed he looked down into the garden he had been so excited to dig and plant back in 1932, when his family had first moved into the house. He looked at the apple tree, now so tall, and sturdy enough for his grandchildren to climb. He remembered the day he and Lizzie had planted it, how their hands had entwined as they held the spade together, joking about how one day they would sit, like Darby and Joan, drinking their tea under the shade of its branches. He looked at the framed photograph sitting on his bedside table. It was an old black and white shot, taken in the garden shortly after they moved in. He, Dot, John, and Lizzie were all posing beside the newly planted tree, smiling at the camera. Dot's eyes, as usual, were screwed up trying to block out the sun, but the funny expression on her face didn't take away from how pretty she looked. She and Lizzie were wearing matching apple green silk dresses with fashionable drop waists. Lizzie had a matching cloche hat on her head, while Dot sported a big green bow in her hair. Lizzie may have broken Valentine's heart, but she had really loved Dot, her little stepdaughter, and had always made sure she was beautifully dressed. For years he had hidden the photo away at the back of his wardrobe, not being able to bear looking at it, not wanting to be reminded of all the heartache. A few years ago he finally fished it out and put it on show. Dot had been thrilled when she saw it. "Oh Dad, what a lovely photo. I remember that day so well. Mum and I looked so nice in those dresses." They had both forgiven Lizzie for hurting them. The years had certainly taken away much of their pain, leaving some happy memories they both treasured.

Valentine still got a bit sad when he thought about the two women he had lost. Lily and Lizzie. The only two women he ever loved who weren't his relatives. Lily and Lizzie had been the loves of his life, and somehow he had never managed to find another. Maybe he just hadn't tried hard enough. He had still been a young man when Lizzie left and there had been a few women over the years who had shown an interest in him, but somehow he had been too scared of getting hurt again. Now he was too old. Just the other day his youngest granddaughter asked him why his eyes were all watery, then asked if he knew that his neck looked just like Timmy, her tortoise's neck! The next morning, catching sight of himself in the mirror while he was shaving with his old cut-throat razor, he chuckled to himself. She was quite right; his old, wrinkled neck did look a bit like a tortoise's neck.

Jean didn't like him using the cut-throat razor, she said he should buy an electric one especially now that his hands were getting a bit shaky. He ignored her. He had shaved the same way all his life and he wasn't going to change now. He still kept up his standards. Clean clothes every day, smart suit and tie and properly polished shoes. Even if he was just at home he dressed up nicely, although sometimes he popped on a warm cardigan over his white or blue shirt, just to keep out the draughts.

He always wore a hat when he left the house. Very necessary, so he could tip it at the ladies as he passed. He knew this was old-fashioned, something that people didn't do these days, but good manners never went unnoticed. That's what his mum had taught him. "Valentine, always behave like a gentleman. Always treat ladies like you would expect people to treat your own sister. Never take advantage of anyone's good nature." His mum's words were deeply ingrained and he had always tried his best to live up to her high standards. Some people thought he was an old fuddy-duddy, but their views of him did not matter.

As he sat contentedly, he could hear murmurs coming from the kitchen where the adults were busy preparing lunch. His five grandchildren were all sitting on the floor, reading their new books and munching on the bars of Cadbury chocolate he had given them.

He smiled contentedly. What a marvellous life he had led. Though not exciting by some people's standards, it had been rich and fulfilling, filled with love, loss, and memories. So many memories.

Valentine George closed his eyes for the last time, happy to know that he was leaving a legacy of love.

He was making room for a new generation, one that would live, love, and suffer loss, just as he had done.

Then they too would die, making space for those to come.

THE END

REFERENCES

The A.B.C. Murders, a novel by Agatha Christie.
(Published 1936)

The Munich Agreement
(Signed in 1938)

The Water Babies, a novel by Charles Kingsley
(Published 1862)

Peter Pan and Wendy, a novel by J.M. Barrie
(Published 1911)

**The Intelligent Woman's Guide to Socialism and
Capitalism,** by George Bernard Shaw
(Published 1928)

Did you enjoy this book? If so, please leave me a review.
I would be delighted to hear from you.

Meet me on my website: www.patbackley.com

AUTHOR BIOGRAPHY

Pat Backley is an English woman, who at the age of 59, decided to become a Kiwi.

She now lives in New Zealand and when not writing, she loves to travel the world (COVID-permitting!). She particularly enjoys spending lots of time in Fiji with her beloved extended Fijian family. She also gardens, paints, reads, and loves activities like interior design, walks on the beach, and socialising.

In short, she lives an ideal existence. However, it hasn't always been so easy, as her memoirs **FROM THERE TO HERE, WITH AN AWFUL LOT IN BETWEEN** will explain.

Pat's other books are:

DAISY (published 2020)
THE SECOND DAISY (published 2021)
FROM THERE TO HERE, WITH AN AWFUL LOT IN BETWEEN (published 2021)

She has also co-authored a best-selling coffee table book entitled:

THE WARRIOR WOMEN PROJECT: A SISTER-HOOD OF IMMIGRANT WOMEN

To learn more about these and her upcoming books visit her website: www.patbackley.com

www.ingramcontent.com/pod-product-compliance
Lightning Source LLC
Chambersburg PA
CBHW021156110726
47900CB00002B/602